Love is a Mysterious Lie

This book is dedicated to my alter ego.

Copyright © 2018 Elizabeth Anna Cunningham
All Rights Reserved.

All rights reserved. No part of this book may be reproduced in any form or by any electronic or mechanical means including information storage and retrieval systems, without permission in writing from the author. The only exception is by a reviewer, who may quote short excerpts in a review.

This book is a work of fiction. Names, characters, places, and incidents either are products of the author's imagination or are used fictitiously. Any resemblance to actual persons, living or dead, events, or locales is entirely coincidental.

Printed in the United States of America

ISBN: 9781717835178

Love is a Mysterious Lie

Elizabeth A. Cunningham

Contents

Contents 4
Chapter 1 5
Chapter 2 12
Chapter 3 19
Chapter 4 28
Chapter 5 35
Chapter 6 42
Chapter 7 50
Chapter 8 58
Chapter 9 67
Chapter 10 76
Chapter 11 85
Chapter 12 94
Chapter 13 100
Chapter 14 107
Chapter 15 116
Chapter 16 123
Chapter 17 130
Chapter 18 140
Chapter 19 146
Chapter 20 153
Chapter 21 160
Chapter 22 168
Chapter 23 176
Chapter 24 184
Chapter 25 192
Chapter 26 201

Chapter 1

Melanie Benton sat up in bed, pondering her marriage and when it started failing. She glanced over at the clock to see it was already the later part of the morning. It was very rare she ever slept past seven most mornings. Her husband, Jim, was out of town this weekend on another business trip to the Florida Keys. Usually she dreaded the days he was absent from the household and out of town on business. Yet, she really wanted to use this time to think over all the issues they had been having. Those issues hadn't become so apparent to her until recently. Her heart was aching at the thought of losing Jim.

She forced herself out of bed and sluggishly walked into the bathroom. Buddy, their chocolate Lab, ran over to the bathroom door and tapped at the doorknob with his nose as she was sitting inside on the toilet. This was always Buddy's way of letting her know he needed to go out. As of late, Melanie has been forgetting about everything else going on around her. She sat there for several minutes, with her underwear and flannel pants at her ankles, as her sad thoughts spiraled out of control. Buddy tapped at the doorknob again, which startled her and snapped her back to reality. After pulling her clothes back up and washing her hands, she left the bathroom to let Buddy out in the backyard.

While she stood outside and looked around, the breeze blew through her hair as she closed her eyes, and her mind drifted back to her wedding day. There she was, walking down the aisle toward Jim, at a beautiful nature preserve on the outskirts of the city. Long, flowing willow trees surrounded them and their guests, as they sat in the white wooden chairs on each side of the walkway. Crystals hung and swung from the trees. The sun was setting and glimmering through the dangling gems, providing a beautiful, calm, and serene backdrop to their ceremony. A friend played Canon in D on the violin nestled beside one of the trees but still visible to everyone.

White rose petals covered the grass to form the aisle toward where Jim was standing. Melanie walked alone, holding a bouquet of white roses. Her white strapless dress was shaped like a mermaid with a sweetheart neckline. The beaded, coral-colored sash around her waist created a stunning focal point. Her long-laced veil slowly dragged behind each step she took, collecting rose petals along the way.

Once their gazes met, Jim saw a twinkle in her eyes. What only took a minute felt like an eternity for Melanie until she met Jim at the end of the aisle. She was overjoyed marrying her best friend and the love of her life. Nothing could go wrong. Her heart fluttered, and butterflies grew in her stomach as she inched closer to him.

He gazed into her eyes as he clutched her hands. The vibration between them was euphoric. A gust of wind blew through the crystals, sounding off jingles around them. Clusters of dark gray clouds rolled in rapidly above everyone. As Sam, the officiant began to speak, a drop of rain landed on the bridge of Jim's nose. It suddenly came down harder. People dashed out of their seats to the overhang in front of the reception hall where Melanie initially walked out.

The wedding planner rushed umbrellas up to Jim and Melanie, as well as the officiant. "They always say it's good luck if it rains on your wedding day," Sam said. Melanie smirked ever so slightly but felt unsettled.

"Do you want to continue this outside, honey, or have them move us inside?" Jim asked his soon-to-be wife.

Melanie remembered the thoughts she had at the time, and she was speechless that the wedding seemed to be ruined already. She sat in silence for a long moment. It felt like she was unable to speak and the feeling overpowered her.

It was difficult for her not to think this was bad luck or a sign, yet she tried not to overthink it and instead embrace it. "Let's brave it out and continue on," she softly replied. "If we get soaked, we get soaked."

They held their umbrellas over their heads and stated their vows to each other. By this time, most people were waiting by the canopy. Melanie's dress was saturated by the end of the ceremony. As they walked back down the aisle holding hands, after being announced as husband and wife, Melanie whispered in Jim's ear, "I'm going to freshen up in the bathroom and will meet you in the changing area I was in earlier."

Melanie picked up her dress with both hands and dashed through the rain to the private restroom on the side of the reception hall. The elegant bathroom was covered with hues of gold, beige, and white. Shiny gold-patterned wallpaper filled the interior of the room. The white and beige-speckled marble slab on the vanity was a beautiful combination with the gold fixtures. She pulled some paper towels from the dispenser and blotted her face. As she looked at herself in the mirror, she felt sadness. Her hair was wet and matted, and makeup was smeared across her face. Clumps of mascara were also settled in the corners of her eyes.

Tears of black ink rolled down her face. She wiped her moist face, but the streams of water would not stop.

"Knock, knock," Grace said outside the locked door. "It's your mother, honey. Everything okay? Can I come in?"

Melanie slowly opened the door to peek through the crack. "Hi, Mom," she said while opening the door.

"Sweetie, are you okay? What's wrong? You just married the love of your life, you should be happy right now."

"Yes, of course I'm happy. I wasn't expecting the rainstorm to pass through. The weather forecast seemed fine when we checked this morning. I don't know, I just feel that maybe this was a bad sign. Did I make a mistake, Mom? And look at me. I look like a train wreck."

Melanie's mother took a handful of paper towels and helped clean her dress. "Honey, you look absolutely stunning. A little rain and smeared makeup doesn't mean it's bad luck. They actually say it's good luck."

"I don't know if I believe that. It doesn't even make sense to me. Why would rain, which ruins your outdoor wedding ceremony, be good luck? I think people are just trying to make light of the situation when they say that. I want statistics proving that it actually brings couples good luck."

Her mother exhaled a loud, audible sigh. "Mel, now you're just being negative. Look on the bright side. That man out there has treated you so well over the years, and you are very lucky to be with him. He's done nothing but take great care of you, and set up a life for you two. Now freshen up, and let's get out to the reception." Her mom walked out and closed the door behind her.

Melanie finished cleaning up, then walked out to begin her new journey.

Her mind then reminisced over their honeymoon; they left the next day for Fiji. Jim's parents paid for an all-inclusive private resort with their own honeymoon suite and infinity pool overlooking the beautiful Fiji waters for a solid seven days. Outside on their private lanai, an outdoor shower was around the corner, surrounded by stones and pebbles. The palm trees were lined up along the perimeter to create extra privacy in their villa. It was paradise for them.

"Babe, who could you possibly be talking to on the phone right now? We just arrived to celebrate our honeymoon only an hour ago."

Melanie inquired to Jim. "It was a business call, just had to take care of a few things." She looked at him in awe and remembered that feeling of being so in love with him, as well as proud to be his wife now. When she walked out to the lanai, she glanced along the horizon, grinning from ear to ear. How did my life get so lucky? She thought to herself.

Their honeymoon consisted of limitless alcohol, skinny dipping, food and sex. Melanie remembered the steamy hot shower they took outside on their private deck. Along with licking whip cream off each other's bodies. Then cleaning off in the pool, naked, while sipping on champagne with fresh raspberries floating in their glasses. Food was delivered buffet style on carts and trays every day to their suite, at least four times a day. They were never hungry. And the alcohol never went empty in their refrigerator, as the staff kept replenishing that as well.

One of the days they were there, they went horseback riding through the waterfalls. It was so peaceful and beautiful, and it was just the two of them. On that day, they tied the horses up to one of the trees, threw off their clothes, and dived off the cliffs into the falls. That was another moment they had a sexual encounter in a public setting. The spontaneity of sex in the beginning of their marriage was blissful and exciting. It all started during their honeymoon and gave Melanie a boost of excitement moving forward for a little while.

Several other couples were staying at the same resort, also on their honeymoon. They connected with some of them but stayed mostly to themselves while they were there. There wasn't a day that went by that they didn't drink and stuff their face with unhealthy food. It was hard not to since everything was all inclusive and unlimited. Even late at night when the restaurants on the resort were closed, the hotel offered room service throughout the wee hours. Most of their honeymoon was spent intoxicated, which probably explained why they were having sex in quite some extravagant and daring places on the island.

At one point, because of how intoxicated they were, they even tried fooling around on the beach in the middle of the day. Neither of them even realized there were several others around, trying to enjoy some peace and quiet by the seaside. The hotel manager had to tell them to take their "business" to their hotel room, or they would be removed from the beach. Melanie was so embarrassed since she had never been in a situation such as that before. However, at the time, the humiliation wore off as quickly as the news came because of her level of intoxication. In the moment, it was well worth the risk. Of course, as soon as they got caught they excused themselves and didn't show face again on the beach the rest of the day.

More than a few times, Melanie observed Jim on his phone. Each time she asked what he was doing, and each time he told her it was "work". She didn't think twice about it since he always had hectic days and he was a very dedicated businessman. Even at home after business hours, he was working on his phone or his laptop. At least that was what he made her believe.

Chapter 2

Melanie's eyes gradually opened. Her mind was wandering all over the place at this point. Was their relationship doomed from the beginning? Overwhelming thoughts were brewing in her imagination again. She saw Buddy out in the distance. The bright green grass was glowing throughout their acres of land. Jim always complained about mowing it, and often would suggest they pay for lawn care. Yet, Melanie did not agree that it was a justifiable expense. The trees that surrounded their patio were blooming shades of purple and pink. In the distance, you could see white specks on the other trees as well. Although Fall was Melanie's favorite time of year, she really enjoyed Spring in New York as well.

Buddy was smelling around the trees and the fallen flower buds when a hummingbird flew by and grabbed his attention. He chased it around the yard while Melanie watched and smiled. She walked out in the grass to grab the light-yellow tennis ball sitting next to one of their lounge chairs. As she was picking it up, Buddy noticed and immediately darted towards her. Right before he reached her, Melanie threw it far into the distance for him to fetch. He quickly chased it, picked it up with his mouth, then ran back to her. She continued throwing it for several minutes until it was obvious that he was wiped out. He slowly walked back towards her, panting heavily. "Let's go get you some water, Buddy."

Melanie walked back inside, feeling anxious and ready to open a bottle of wine. The stress and anxiety had been heavily weighing down on her. Dark, heavy bags were noticeable under her eyes and her skin was quite pale. She had lost several pounds over the past few weeks from eating less and less. Her body was frail and thin, where it looked as if she were dying from some sort of serious illness. Her friends even told her she looked sick. She didn't realize how bad she looked to others until she looked at some photos of herself from several months ago in her phone. It was hard to believe how alive she looked months ago compared to today.

The stress was not only affecting her internally, but more visibly externally. Nothing seemed to work to calm her nerves or slow down her heart rate. Exercising wasn't helping and at this point she lost all motivation for that. Normally, when she took Buddy on long walks it helped ease her mind. Even just being in nature with fresh air or near the water used to help. Lately, nothing like that had worked to ease her stress. It hadn't worked in months, and only seemed to be getting worse.

She headed back towards the master bedroom. As she passed through the kitchen, she realized she still hadn't eaten. She walked past the fridge, and grabbed a banana from the fruit bowl on the counter. An orange fell out of the bowl and onto the floor. Buddy scampered over to attempt a quick snatch. "No!" She yelled in his direction. He ran off, with his tail tucked, and plopped back down on his down and feather filled bed. Melanie picked up the orange and placed it back into the basket before opening the refrigerator. She stared at all the open shelves and empty drawers.

One lonely Corona Light bottle was situated in the middle. The refrigerator light shined on it so brightly, that it called her attention immediately. It wasn't like her to drink in the middle of the day, but she was not in a good headspace to care right now. She reached in to snag it, before opening the drawer next to the fridge. Frantically she shuffled around the random silverware, rubber bands, paperclips and other items. The search for a bottle opener seemed endless. Then she suddenly could hear "Ahhhh" of Angels singing in her head as she located it.

Snap. The bottle cap flung onto the counter. The sound of a crisp, fresh, cold beer opening was so pleasing to her ears. Melanie tossed the contraption back into the junk drawer, and slammed it shut with her hip. The bottle cap remained lifeless and still on the counter next to the coffee maker. After she left the kitchen, Buddy rose from his bed and sniffed around where the orange had tumbled earlier. He located a couple of crumbs and licked them up faster than he could even recognize what they were. Nothing else seemed interesting enough for him, so he meandered off.

Melanie stared off into the living room, like a deer in headlights. In her mind, the memory of her words "How did my life get so lucky?" kept replaying. To think, here they were in a much different position now. It was so confusing to her why things had shifted so dramatically for them since they got married a couple years ago. There may have been some signs that something was changing for Jim, but Melanie was so infatuated with him that she didn't recognize any of it. As she was staring off into space, she thought of all the times Jim seemed a little off or vague when it came to his phone. He would constantly flip his phone over and face down. It was always on silent or vibrate, in his pocket or the bathroom. Pretty much anywhere he was, his phone was attached to his hip. She had never felt the need to snoop on his phone but now she was starting to wonder.

Melanie walked back to her bedroom, with Buddy now by her side. The king bedspread was freshly laid out across the bed, with a clump in the right corner where she normally slept. Without Jim in the bed, his side was still made perfectly without a crease. Shades of bright white, pinks and purple tones were spread out on the comforter. She slumped down on the bed, snuggled into her bundle, and clenched the cold beer in her hands. As she sat up against the grey cushy headboard, she took a sip of the beer. The liquid tingled and burned as it glided down her throat to her stomach. In an instant, she burped from the air in her swallow.

While drinking the beer, a rush of adrenaline took over her. She chugged the remainder of her beer, then changed into yoga pants and threw a hoodie over her t-shirt. It had been a long time since she went into the city, let alone by herself. She grabbed her keys, purse, cell phone and "You are a Badass" book she recently started reading before she was out the door. Melanie speedily headed towards the train station as if she had a meeting to make.

The train arrived five minutes after she sat down on the bench waiting for it. After getting on and selecting her seat, she started reading her book until she reached her stop in the city. Melanie shoved the book back into her purse, got off the train and walked from block to block. She didn't stop, until she got to Central Park. The adrenaline began to slow down in her blood stream as she walked farther in the park, into the peaceful nature around her. While strolling through, she found a bench overlooking a lake. Right as she was about to sit down, she realized she had only eaten a banana today.

Melanie moved along through the city streets again and located a hot dog stand. There were so many memories she had at these hot dog stands with her Dad when she was little. Each time she traveled to the city with her family, her Dad would sneak her off to get a hot dog and pretzel for them to share. The smell of the food and the city brought back those fond memories. She ordered a hot dog and a Coke, then sat on a ledge so she could people watch and reminisce.

There were thousands of people running all around her. Some people were rushing past, while several others stopped repetitively to snap a photo. The number of tourists in the city was quite impressive. As she was getting lost people-watching, she looked up towards the sky and at the buildings. The reflection of the sunshine was bouncing off the buildings and mirroring onto others. The city was so beautiful, she thought to herself. Melanie closed her eyes, while still looking up towards the sky. She could feel the sun basking on her skin.

Soon after, she snapped out of her daydream to finish her hot dog, then decided to stop over at Starbucks. There was a coffee shop at almost every corner in the city. When she walked by, the aroma of coffee took over her senses and forced a smile on her face. There was something just by the smell of coffee that made her feel more alert and happier, before even having her first sip. She waited in line for several minutes until she reached the counter to order a latte. "Melanie," the barista called out. She picked up her beverage, and headed out the door for more city exploring. Even though she lived close to the city, she felt like continuing her adventures as a tourist for the day.

Melanie walked outside with her Starbucks in hand, and headed towards Rockefeller Center. She paid her ticket to view the city from the rooftop deck. After making her way up to the top, she stood outside, overlooking Central Park and the lake she saw earlier. The scenery was breathtaking from that point of view. The people in the ice-skating rink looked like little ants, and the skyscrapers were now at her eye level and below. She sipped on her coffee, which had cooled down, as she took in all the sights. There were several people and couples surrounding her, making her feel slightly cramped. She noticed a couple nearby having a serious fight over something but it was hard to make out what they were arguing over. Melanie thought to herself, it is such a beautiful day, with a spectacular view. What could possibly be so important to fight over right now? She shook her head in disbelief.

Once her coffee cup was almost empty, she headed back down to the streets towards the Museum of Modern Art. While walking past each building, she tossed the now hollow paper cup into one of the trash cans adjacent to the museum. When she walked inside and paid the fee, she moved from one gallery to the next in awe of the artwork surrounding her. Each painting that was catching her eye, kept her from moving on to the next for several minutes at a time. The colors and talent in each creation were mesmerizing. She spent a couple hours in the museum until she got her art "fix"; then left to head back to the train station and travel home.

Chapter 3

Melanie arrived at Kristin's New Year's Eve party, assuming she would most likely be depressed the entire night as the single, lonely gal. There were high hopes she may kiss someone at midnight, but she knew that probably wouldn't happen. Many of Kristin's male friends all seemed to have girlfriends each time she saw them. Yet, this time around, a few of the guys came with single male friends, too.

Melanie noticed Jim the instant she walked into Kristin's house. He was chatting with a tall, beautiful blonde. Her initial thoughts were that the woman was a model, and Jim was probably her boyfriend. He looked so handsome wearing a charcoal colored suit with a blue collared shirt underneath the jacket. It brought more of the blue out in his eyes. They were beautiful. His shiny golden-brown perfect hair fell along the side of his face with a slight wave. Melanie wanted to feel the smoothness of his flawlessly shaven skin. His jawbones looked strong and tough like his physique. He was sexy as hell to her, and one of the hottest guys she has seen around in a long time.

Melanie continued walking through the house to find Kristin. She noticed Jim caught her staring at him as she walked by. They shared a moment of curiosity through each other's eyes before she stepped around the corner. Kristin was in the kitchen setting out more food and drinks. "You've done a great job decorating the place. Where's my party hat?" said Melanie.

"Thanks. Yeah, I was up all day making hors d'oeuvres and buying all the decorations. I am exhausted right now but the party is just getting started, so I need to get this done. All the goodies are over there on the table," Kristin said pointing to the table, but the direction aimed straight to Jim and the blonde.

"Oh, you mean right next to that hot guy and his girlfriend?"

"No, here inside the kitchen. Oh, that guy is Jim. He is Derek's buddy."

Melanie nodded as she listened intently. "Who is that girl he is talking to? Are they a couple?"

"That's Adriana. She is a model from Europe and knows someone else here or something like that. I met her about thirty minutes ago. I have no idea if they know each other or not, but I don't believe they are together like that."

"Oh ok, well can I help with anything? We have a few more hours until we ring in the New Year and you need to have some fun, too."

"No, go enjoy yourself. I'll be around in a few minutes. I have a few more things to get done first."

Melanie grabbed the bottle of Tanqueray and a tonic water. If she wanted to feel better about herself and to possibly muster up the courage to talk to this Jim guy, or any guy for that matter, then she needed to drink up. Liquid courage, she thought to herself. She grabbed a red plastic cup and poured the gin halfway up the cup, then filled the rest of the cup with tonic water. Before deciding to go back in the room where he was, she thought a shot or two should do the trick, giving her even more nerve. Melanie took ahold of the Patron, and took a couple swigs straight from the bottle.

"Woo!"

"Wow Mel, you are quite the drinker, huh?" Kristin laughed, but she also seemed impressed at the same time.

"Yeah well, if I want to grow some balls to walk up to that Jim guy, and impress him, then I need to be a little tipsy at first." They both laughed.

"Well, good luck then!"

In the other room, Jim was still having a conversation with Adriana. Melanie walked out of the kitchen holding her drink and immediately locked eyes with Jim again. Adriana kept brushing her body against his and flipping her hair around, seeking the attention back to her. Her hair looked to be platinum-blonde, and not natural at all. It was obvious she was turning him on. Jim's eyes had determination in them as he looked back at her. Her blonde curls bounced around while she flirted with him.

Melanie was comparing herself to the beautiful blonde and felt pathetic. She looked around to scope out the other men at the party, figuring it was probably a lost cause with Jim. There wasn't much of a selection, since most of the guys had girls on their arms. It was hard to tell who was taken or who was just mingling with women. She felt alone and down on herself in that moment.

Melanie walked away with her head down in utter disappointment in herself. It was rather pitiful if others were watching. The satin dress she wore swayed with every motion her legs took towards the sofa. She sat down, then crossed her legs like a lady.

A man was sitting right next to her. His hair was a little scruffy, with dirty blonde flickers of color. It covered most of his forehead. His eyes were a deep chocolate brown, which did not strike her as unique in any way. She did however like his face; he had this puppy dog expression to it. She didn't realize she was studying him for so long until he gave her a look for staring at him without speaking.

"Hi, I'm Kevin," he said while putting his arm around Melanie.

"Oh, Hello. Sorry I didn't mean to stare. I'm Melanie."

"Very nice to meet you Melanie. Are you here with anyone?"

"Well, not exactly. I stopped by to enjoy the New Year's party with some friends. How about yourself?"

"Nope. Not with anyone. So just to stop by? Are you that busy of a woman?" He sarcastically asked.

"Well, I mean, I...."

Kevin cuts her off mid-sentence, "Listen, I really just want to know if you are a single or not? I need a girl to kiss tonight at midnight to make my ex jealous. You may be the lucky winner for me. You in?" Melanie felt uncomfortable and was speechless at his cockiness. Also, at his lack of manners. She managed to get out a few words.

"Um, yeah, my boyfriend should be here soon. You might want to move on to some other woman who is "lucky" enough to be in your presence."

Kevin looked at her astonished. "Boyfriend? You said you weren't here with anyone…"

She had to find another way to escape from this conversation. Jim noticed what was happening and saw that she looked stressed. He immediately walked over and squeezed right in the middle of Kevin and herself. "Hey sweetie."

Melanie smirked, "Oh hi, um honey." Kevin had a puzzled look on his face, then quickly took off.

"I saw you from across the room; you looked like you needed someone to save you from that dude."

"Oh, did I? Well, I was doing fine, thank you. Since when did you have time to glance over at myself with your girlfriend all over you?" Melanie didn't mean to come off so blunt, but the alcohol was kicking in.

"Well, look at you. Been observing me too, huh? That's Adriana. She's not my girlfriend, but a lovely lady at that. To tell you the truth, talking to her was like talking to my friend's daughter, who is around ten mind you. I was hoping for a more intelligent conversation this evening. When she was talking on and on about her modeling career, I glanced over at you and darted away from her as quickly as I could. It was my escape from that conversation. I should be thanking you."

I knew she was a model, Melanie said in her mind. "Well, you're welcome then," she grinned. Adriana interrupted them for a moment, attempting to mark her territory on Jim. However, he did not play into it as she expected. She very quickly moved her beet red face out the situation and went straight to the bar.

They continued talking for hours and it seemed they were hitting it off. Their conversations consisted of childhood, family, and even their favorite flavor of ice cream. He was acting like such a gentleman to her, jumping up to refill her drink each time she was low. Either he was being a gentleman, or Jim was trying to get her drunk enough to get in her pants. Melanie didn't seem too worried about that in the moment. At this point, she was just happy to have found a man to possibly kiss at midnight. And a good one at that. At one moment during their conversation, some drama unfolded with Adriana. Melanie was so tipsy that she couldn't focus on what was happening, but people were yelling in some areas and others were gasping in shock. Then suddenly Adriana and her friend were out the door.

The countdown from ten was already there. And just like that, it was officially the new year. "Happy New Year Melanie."

"Happy New Year Jim." Jim leaned in for a kiss. Melanie was in heaven. She was on cloud nine and thought she just met the man of her dreams. The end of the night felt so perfect. Shortly after they rung in the New Year together, as to grab ahold of the euphoric high she experienced, she decided to call it a night. Even though the night was so blissful, and she didn't want it to end, but it seemed more appropriate to do so, in hopes he will ask her out on a proper date soon.

The following day rolled around rather quickly, being that most of it was spent with a hangover. Even dealing with that, it was hard for Melanie to avoid looking at her phone the entire day, hoping to hear from him again. Twelve hours passed since they last saw each other, before Jim texted Melanie.

"Good afternoon beautiful. Meeting you last night was a breath of fresh air. How are you feeling?" Several minutes passed before Melanie noticed he had sent her a message, since she was trying to keep herself occupied. Once she saw his name on her phone, her heart palpitated in excitement.

She immediately responded with a slight lie, "I'm feeling pretty great, actually. And meeting you was quite wonderful for me. How are you feeling?"

Jim responded a few minutes later, "I'm doing fine myself. You free later?"

She jumped up in excitement, after seeing he was possibly asking her on a date. That was much sooner than she anticipated. Yet, she didn't want to come off as desperate or boring that she didn't have plans on New Year's Day. "I did have plans with some friends, but I believe they had something come up," she lied again. Jim didn't respond for several hours at that point, which had her over-thinking that maybe he lost interest or made other plans.

During her detox to try to and rid the hangover, he responded back. "Great. I'd love to take you out on a date if you'd like? Ever been to Gramercy Tavern? Let's meet there at 9:30 PM."

The thrill built up inside her body. What am I going to wear? How should I do my hair? What shoes should I wear? She was already driving herself crazy with her thoughts. Since it was in the dead middle of winter, there were only so many outfit options to wear. Scarves and boots were her favorite accessory during this time of year. It was still quite early before their date, but the adrenaline had her frantically rummaging through her closet.

Yellow dress or black dress? Jeans or a sexy skirt? Long sleeve shirt or short sleeve? Heavy jacket with less clothing or lighter jacket with more clothing? Boots with heels or without? The options seemed endless in her kooky mind. Clothes were piling up on the floor and on the bed in her studio apartment. Buddy, at only six months old, saw the mound of clothes on the floor and within no time he jumped on top. He moved them around with his paws to make the perfect accumulation to lay on.

Melanie finally chose what she wanted to wear after ferociously searching through and trying on several different outfits. She settled on something comfortable and sexy. Dark blue skinny jeans, with an inviting but casual beige shirt, followed with a scarf and tan heeled ankle boots. In addition, she added a blazer. Time could not pass fast enough before she would be taking the subway to the restaurant.

All dressed up earlier than expected, she dozed off into a cat nap. Which turned into a few hours of deep sleep without her realizing it. Completely unexpected. By the time she woke up, she was rushing to finish getting ready since she was running late for the subway.

It was already nine o'clock. She took a couple shots of cucumber flavored vodka she had in her freezer to calm her nerves. As she touched up her makeup and spritzed a couple sprays of perfume on her body, she rushed down the stairs. Since it was too late for the subway, she whistled for a taxi. It was always easy hailing a taxi in the city; they were everywhere. Within thirty seconds, a yellow cab pulled up next to her.

She dove in. "Gramercy Tavern, please." The cab driver didn't say anything in return and drove until reaching the destination. Melanie arrived close to 9:45 PM, which was fifteen minutes later than she was scheduled to meet Jim. When the driver pulled up to the restaurant, Melanie handed him a twenty-dollar bill before rushing out. There he was, standing at the door, looking as handsome as she remembered from last night. He was wearing black pants with a matching sport coat. The shirt underneath was a light purple shade that matched the pocket square in his jacket. Jim grabbed both of Melanie's hands, pulled her in, and gave her a passionate kiss. The rest was history.

Chapter 4

Melanie awoke from her daydreams of reminiscing about the past. It was nice for her to ruminate over the feelings she had from the first day she met Jim. When she thought back to those days, it helped her appreciate how much of a lucky woman she really was to have a wonderful man like him in her life. After all those thoughts and feeling the butterflies again, it made her realize how much she wanted to save their marriage.

She logged on the computer and looked up marriage counselors in the area. The best solution for them right now seemed to be counseling. Next to the computer on their desk, sat a notepad decorated with lilies. She opened the desk drawer to grab a pen and write down the counselor information.

The best time to make the appointment would be Monday, when Jim would be back in town again. He was arriving on Sunday evening this week. She picked up the phone to call Mrs. Samson to set up the appointment, and confirmed it for 6:30 PM the following Monday evening.

A couple days had passed since she had heard from Jim. He last spoke to her on Tuesday when she dropped him off at the airport. Not texting or talking on the phone to each other, felt like ages since they had any conversation. She was debating if she should call him or not. Sometimes he got annoyed by phone calls since he told her before how often he gets busy while traveling. That had made her nervous to pick up the phone to call her own husband. Right as she convinced herself to call him, the telephone rings. Melanie doesn't recognize the number, but still picks it up to answer it. "Hello?" She asked in confusion.

All she could hear were several voices and tones in the background. Someone must've butt-dialed me, she thought to herself. However, there was something about that call that seemed a little off to her, but she couldn't put her finger on it. The call began distracting her thoughts so much that she forgot to even contact Jim.

Slowly but surely, she pulled herself off the chair at the computer and migrated to the couch. The hair on her head that was once in a bun earlier in the day, was now a droopy, tangling mess. It blended in well with her attire, which was a tank top with holes around the armpits, no bra, and torn, faded cotton shorts. Who am I trying to impress anyway? She mumbled to herself.

One commercial on the television changed to the next and so on as she flipped through a variety of channels. Nothing was catching her eye nor was anything intriguing enough to stop the clicking. Her brain seemed to be on mute. A throw pillow was stuffed under her cheek as she laid down sideways on the couch. The last channel on television she landed on was a chick flick. It was some kind of romantic movie that looked familiar to her. This was not quite the genre she was in the mood for, so she kept flipping through more stations. Finally, she stopped on the History Channel. In her mind, learning something may be the best solution to keep her attention off other things for now. "Oh good. I can learn about Medieval Torture Devices. This may come in handy someday," she laughed out loud.

Suddenly, her phone rang again from the same number that called her earlier, but no one was on the other line this time when she answered. "Hello? Who is this?" She heard a man's voice, which for a second sounded like Jim's. As well as a female's voice. Then audible moans and sighs. What the hell is going on?! She furiously thought to herself. Suddenly, the weird gut and uncomfortable feelings formed in her stomach. Melanie clicked to end the phone call, then immediately called Jim. His phone went straight to voicemail. Now, she was panicking.

After three unsuccessful phone calls to Jim, she leaves him a voicemail to call her back as soon as possible. Following a text message to her voicemail. As the minutes of silence passed, the anxiety grew inside her like a balloon about to explode. She decided to call the number back that initially called her in the first place, but no one answered the call. However, the voice recording stated "Adriana Santos." When she hung up the phone, she bounced up so fast to jump on her MacBook. Her fingers couldn't even type fast enough to keep up with the swirling thoughts in her head.

To start with, she entered in the Google webpage. In Google box, she typed Adriana's first and last name, then clicked on images. The first thing that popped up was that she was a model from Brazil. There's no way this was the same woman from the phone call. Why would she accidentally call me? How would Jim even know her? And then it hits her. The photos showed Adriana with long brown hair, until Melanie stumbled across an older one where she used to have blonde hair. "Oh, my gosh! Was this the same woman from the New Year's party I met Jim at?!" She can't help but talk out loud to herself after seeing those images.

All sorts of mind-boggling thoughts are running through her brain. There was so much confusion as to what was happening here with Jim and Adriana. She didn't even know what to do or where to begin with what she was discovering. Nausea developed in her stomach over the thought of Jim having an affair. And with that woman. Her. The same woman that made her feel insecure at that party where they met several years ago. Has this been going on since then? She asked herself, amongst several other questions.

Melanie's heart was racing as she picked up the phone to call Jim again, and the call was still going straight to voicemail. Even when she called Adriana's phone, it did the same thing. This was driving her practically insane, craving answers to all these questions. She paced around the house, not knowing what to do with herself. Her thoughts escalated so far out of control, that she ran to the toilet to vomit. It was hard for her to do anything else at this point, but to overthink everything. The silence from him was killing her.

Buddy could sense something was wrong and kept pawing at Melanie as she laid back down on the couch, crying uncontrollably. "Not now, Buddy," she cried. He stood there staring at her, unable to comprehend what she meant by what she said. Her arms were above her head, with one covering her eyes. Buddy licked her arm, then laid down on the floor next to her. The crying was overpowering and wasn't slowing down in any way. Sadness, depression and anxiety overcame her entire body.

The sun rose the following morning and the birds chirped as the peak of sunlight was visible. Melanie woke up in a panic from Buddy barking at the squirrels through the window. She vastly sat up like a prairie dog, instantly confused and looking around; still in a sleep haze. I guess I passed out from all the crying and drinking I did after that call. She thought in her mind. Once she came to, she picked up her phone and realized it was dead. She ran into the bedroom to charge her phone. After turning it on while it was charging, a voicemail alert popped up. It was from Jim.

"Hey babe, saw you called. Sorry I was tied up in meetings all day. I'm back at the hotel now ordering room service and calling it a night. I'll talk to you in the morning. Love you." The anxiety in Melanie's chest and stomach quickly cleared up. Instant relief overcame her body and soul. Maybe I was exaggerating the situation? Did that call happen yesterday? I remember having a few beers, but maybe I had more than I realized? She talked herself out of the idea that Jim was cheating on her, and that most of yesterday was probably just brain fog since she hasn't been eating much lately.

While her phone was still charging, she threw on different clothes and walked into the kitchen to make breakfast. A pounding headache was throbbing in the forefront of her head. She pulled out Illy coffee from the pantry to brew a pot of it. Scoop after scoop, she dumped the ground coffee into the filter and filled up the coffee maker with water to the line it suggested for four cups; then pressed start. While it was brewing, she pulled out a frying pan to make scrambled eggs and bacon. Her appetite somewhat appeared this morning. When she walked over to the fridge, searching for the bacon, Buddy approached her as soon as he heard her pick up the package.

The frying pan sizzled with the butter that was melting in it. She pulled out a few sticky pieces of bacon and threw them into the pan. Loud crackle and pop sounds echoed in the kitchen. The aroma was now a mixture of coffee beans and bacon. Buddy's tongue stuck out as he salivated to the scents. She opened the cabinet next to the refrigerator and pulled out her 'Namaste' mug. Coffee quickly filled up halfway in the clear pot, streaming of warm and fresh coffee liquid. She poured a full cup in her mug, before adding French vanilla creamer in it. Ahhhh. She said with her first sip.

As the bacon hissed, her phone text message alert sounded. She walked over to look at it and saw that it was Jim. "Hey baby. Did you see I called you last night? I'm headed into more meetings now. Love you." It was in that moment she realized she completely forgot to respond to his voicemail earlier. Holding her phone in one hand, and coffee in the other, she tried multitasking and texting him back one handed. Hot coffee proceeded to spilled over the almost full mug and onto the floor which then splashed on her toes. "Dammit!" She screamed.

Buddy was already by her side, licking up as much coffee as he could before he realized how hot it was. The phone drops out of her hand as she bent down to wipe up the coffee. Now, she was downright frustrated. She picked the phone back up and replied to Jim. "Yes, I did this morning, my phone died overnight because I forgot to charge it.

Have a good day. I love you too." A slight burning smell overcame her senses as she put the phone back down on the counter. "Oh, shoot!" She yelled while rushing over to the frying pan. The bacon had turned a dark black crisp on one end. Melanie reached for a fork and carefully took the strips out of the greasy pan to throw on a plate with a paper towel.

The paper towel immediately soaked in all the grease. Making the eggs now seemed like an annoyance to her. Wheat bagels were sitting neatly wrapped on the counter next to the toaster. She opened the package to take one out and tossed it in the toaster. Once the bagel popped up and was a slight, crusty brown, she placed it on a plate with a few pieces of the burnt bacon. After slabbing on butter to each toasted side of the bagel, Melanie recognized the newspaper wasn't sitting on the table like it normally was. The newspaper was still sitting outside the front door of her entrance steps. Normally, she liked to read the newspaper while eating breakfast and drinking coffee. The newspaper had piled up on the front steps for the last several days; and was soggy and humid from the rain. It went straight into the trash.

Melanie sat at the breakfast table eating her bagel and sipping on her coffee, re-thinking what happened the day before. Something doesn't feel right in her gut, even though Jim stated he was in meetings all day prior. Why would I get a couple calls from that number and not hear from him all day? I swear I heard his voice in the background. And he left me a voicemail at 11:30 PM, which he has never had meetings that late. Was that Adriana that called me? The thoughts kept spinning in her mind.

Chapter 5

Jim rushed back to the resort for a little action with Adriana before his next meeting. She was patiently waiting for him in her black silk robe. Underneath, she had on black lace panties with a matching lace bra that was exposing her nipples. In anticipation, she laid on the bed with a glass of Dom Perignon. She reached over for a chocolate covered strawberry off the polished stainless-steel tray that rested on the nightstand.

While she was nibbling on the strawberry, and leaning against the soft white headboard, she glanced over at the clock. "12:36 PM and he's still keeping me waiting. This is ridiculous," she mumbled to herself while shaking her head. Out of boredom, she picked up her phone to call Melanie, then hung up when she noticed Jim storming through the front door of the suite.

"Adriana! Darling! I'm so sorry to keep you waiting...", before he was able to finish his sentence, Adriana was already standing in front of his face in her 3-inch black stilettos, with her finger up against his lips, hushing him. She kissed him with the half-eaten strawberry still in her mouth; then passed it through to his mouth. Sweetly, and passionately, gently gliding her tongue over his. Jim slightly moaned and sighed. She brushed her body closer against his, feeling the excitement throughout his body.

Jim moaned louder, while Adriana strutted over to her champagne, then slowly strolled back towards him looking straight into his eyes without blinking. His eyes gleamed of hunger. She took a sip and kissed him, sharing the sweet taste in her mouth with him. The passion was exuding from their bodies. He grabbed her body, and forced her onto the bed. Adriana took back control, and grabbed his arms to flip him over on his back. Jim's pants were about to burst from eagerness.

As he laid there salivating at her, she slowly untied the robe and allowed it to fall to the floor. She touched her body, gliding her hands over her breasts and down to her lower region. Jim couldn't contain his excitement any longer. He forced his way up and over to her. As he ripped off his pants, he kissed all over her body. His tongue slid down below her navel and with his teeth, he bit her laced panties. Slowly, he pulled them all the way down to her stilettos. She lifted one leg to kick them off while his tongue skimmed its way back up her legs. Before Adriana could blink her eyes again, she moaned in passion as Jim was tasting her.

Adriana fell against the wall, unable to take the pleasure much more. Jim stood up, grabbed her perfectly shaped butt and lifted her up, then wrapped her legs around his body. He turned around and tossed her body back on the bed and took her right there. Loud, exhaled sighs released from their bodies in bliss. Her neck contorts, lifting her chin high in the air right before she has her first orgasm. The gratification turns Jim on even more. He flipped her body over on her stomach, and kissed each vertebra down her spine. Both of their soft, deep moans are now more audible tones. His lips continued down to her buttocks, as he spread open her legs even further.

While she felt his tongue tasting her again, she clenched the sheets tightly in her hands. Right as she was about to have her second orgasm, he slid himself back inside her. Both of his hands grabbed the sides of her hips as he pulled her body further into the air, and closer to his pelvis. Faster and harder, he moved in and out of her, then released himself into gratification. Jim moaned profoundly before his body collapsed on top of hers. Adriana took one of his hands, and held it tightly. Every time they had sex, she felt a more intense connection between them. Jim pulled himself out of her, and rolled over onto the bed.

They both immediately fell into a peaceful sleep. After an hour passed, Jim's phone incessantly vibrated from a call. He sent the call to voicemail when he realized it was Melanie. The loud buzzing sound against the nightstand woke up Adriana. When she turned over, she realized her phone was laying under the comforter. She unlocked the phone to look at her call history and noticed that her phone somehow dialed Melanie again.

Adriana forgot that her impatience waiting on Jim earlier that day, gave her this urge to confront Melanie about their affair; in hopes she would leave Jim. The call history showed two outgoing calls to Melanie; and one those lasted a couple of minutes. Which meant it went to her voicemail or Melanie picked up the phone.

"Who was that that just called you?" She asked Jim.

"Just my wife again. She's called me a few times after we fell asleep." As they are speaking, his phone vibrated again from a text message that came through.

He read the messages from Melanie. "Jim, what is going on? I've tried calling and can't seem to get in touch with you. I got a weird call from an unknown number and I swear I heard your voice in the background. Call me back as soon as possible!"

Jim frantically sat up. "What the hell? Did you call my wife? Because she just texted me that a call came through to her and she heard me in the background. She's freaking out now! How did you get her number? Are you trying to blow my cover Adriana?!" He angrily expressed to her.

"No! Calm down. I didn't contact her, so I don't know what she's talking about. I was with you the whole time," she lied to him.

"Well, I don't know what the hell happened, but I'll figure it out later," Jim sternly replied.

Adriana watched his sexy jawline move as he spoke to her. She was too mesmerized focusing on his chiseled chest and jaw to care what he was saying to her in that moment.

"Alright, babe. I need to head out," he uttered while he got up searching for his boxer briefs.

As he was putting his suit back on, Adriana commented, "Oh, I didn't realize you'd have to run off so quickly. Are we still meeting later for dinner?" While putting his sport coat back on, he responded, "Yes, babe. I'll text you later." Then instantly walked out of the door after picking up his mobile phone.

Something didn't feel right to Adriana. She had a feeling he may take a rain check on her. I wonder if he's meeting other women here, too, she thought to herself. Lying there in silence, thinking of that possibility was making her feel foolish. The feeling inside was causing her so much stress. For a moment, she even felt like he may be using her. After briefly dwelling on the situation, she got up to take a shower. The glass shower walls sparkled as she stepped on the grey stoned pebbles. They felt good on her feet, as if she were getting small massages.

The remote to the television in the vanity mirror was sitting on top of the counter. She wanted to watch something to distract all her thoughts but was already wet in the shower. After cleaning herself up, she hopped out and turned on the TV. The news channel was the first thing to pop-up. "Might as well catch up on current events," she said out loud to herself.

While drying off, she glanced over her shoulder to look out the window. The clear blue water was twinkling from the sunshine. "I can't let this ruin such a beautiful day. And it's not very often I get to come to a resort for a relaxing staycation and not work," she said to herself. Adriana walked back into the bedroom to search for her pink and black bathing suit that was stuffed somewhere in her duffle bag. Once she located it, she threw it on, with a white sheer cover-up. "Where is my sun hat?" She took a moment to track down her suntan lotion before finding her hat squashed under more clothes.

The seagulls squawked in excitement and flew into the slight breeze outside. Beach chairs and umbrellas surrounded a large section of the beach. The lounge chairs were topped with bright blue cushions and canopies overtop for shade. People looked happy and truly relaxed by the water. A lifeguard sat outside his tower, watching over the beach and the people in the water. His perfectly tan, shaped chest glistened from the sunshine as beads of sweat dripped down his upper body. Meow. Adriana's body fluttered for a second when she noticed him.

She trekked through the powder sand towards one of the lounge chairs. On her way there, she saw a towel stand with two young gentlemen behind the counter. "Good afternoon ma'am. How many towels would you like? Do you have your room key?" Adriana searched in her small pink bag for her room key and handed it over to them. "Two please." One of the guys took her key to scan, while the other one handed over two towels. "Please return them here when you are done using them. Have a great day!" She smiled at them and walked away with both blue and white striped towels.

There were a few unused lounge chairs near the lifeguard stand that she wandered towards to set up shop. As she put one towel down on the cushioned chair, she rolled up the other one to use as a pillow. Then she searched in her bag for her iPod and headphones. Once she got settled in and was lying down, the music soothed and relaxed her body so easily, that she dozed off. Her bronzed skin, slowly turned darker as the hours passed.

The waves were crashing down into the sand so peacefully. In the distance, grey clouds were developing into larger clumps. They continued growing, and moving swiftly towards the resort, blocking the sun. Several people packed up their things and walk back towards the resort. The sky was gloomy and dark. A few rain drops landed on Adriana's body, which woke her up suddenly. "Whoa, how long was I out?" She asked herself. As she sat up from the chair, she looked out to the water, which now looked murky from the reflection of the grey clouds. There wasn't much energy left in her body to get up and move. The rain fell harder and faster, while she sat up in the chair, lifeless.

Chapter 6

Melanie picked up the phone without checking the caller ID and answered, confused since it was a little after midnight and she was half asleep. The first thing she heard was a woman giggling again on the other end of the line. When she looked down at the phone, she saw it was the same number that called her before, where she thought she heard Jim's voice. She repeatedly said, "Hello?"

Finally, a female voice responded. "Is this Melanie?"

Melanie felt anxious before responding, "Yes, speaking. Who is this?" The woman was still laughing, and Melanie could hear a man in the background again. It sounded like he was tickling her or something since she kept laughing at something. The woman was clearly intoxicated by the sound of her voice.

"There's a man you know quite well, that I also know quite well. I want you to know, I am madly in love with him." The woman stated.

"Jim? You said Jim??" Melanie repeated, anxiously awaiting a response.

"Yes - Jim. You got it. He is with me right now as a matter of fact." She kept talking and mumbling, but Melanie couldn't make out everything she was saying and was unable to handle it any longer. She hung up the phone and threw it on the bed. All kinds of thoughts were running through her head. Reaching for the phone, she picked it up from the bed and checked the caller ID again. Without realizing before that it was Adriana's number. Her stomach started churning. Tears filled her eyes. It was hard for her to comprehend why this woman would call her and act so nonchalant about something so devastating and hurtful. If she knew he was married, how could she do such a thing? Questions kept running through her head; as well as confusion. She reached for a tissue box that sat on one of their bedside tables.

The following morning, Jim woke up hungover and disorderly. "Damn, Adriana! Did you call my wife again last night? She will rip me a new one for this! All these texts she sent throughout the night and after what happened the day before; it seems she knows what is going on now thanks to you. It was already a close enough call from yesterday, but you apparently ripped that band-aide off for us. Much appreciated."

Adriana casually responded, "Oh, it was just a joke babe. Calm down. I don't even remember what I said or if she even answered. Do you? We were both drunk and were just being playful. I'm sure you can come up with a good lie that I am one of your clients you were helping or something. Anyways, you told me you were going to leave her. So maybe this will push things along for you. I'm tired of going back and forth like we have for years. It's time you divorce her and be with me already. I've waited long enough, Jim."

"Baby, you know things are hard right now. It's not that easy and I need time. Now I need to figure out a good lie to get myself out of this tangled mess you got me into. I'll find a way. Maybe next week I will tell my wife I have a meeting out of town and we can meet in Boston for a nice little getaway. What do you say?" He mentioned, hoping to satisfy her enough to buy him more time.

"Well, that would be nice, I guess. But seriously, get on the divorce thing already, Jim. You've had plenty of time."

He let out a sigh of frustration, "Okay, I'll call or text you later tonight after I get into the city. I need to do a few things before catching my flight. Love you." He gathered his things while speaking to her.

"I love you too, Jim. I will miss you terribly as always. One more quickie?"

She unbuttoned her white sheer blouse she slept in the night before. Her breasts were now exposed with no bra covering them. She knew exactly how to turn him on. Then, she placed her hand on her neck and slid it down between her breasts, and continued down in slow motion to her cotton shorts underwear. Jim got so turned on when she touched herself. He grabbed her body and threw her on the bed, in a sexy playful way. Only fifteen minutes passed before he was out the door.

Jim hopped into his black Ford Mustang of a rental car, and sped off. After a couple turns, he arrived at a boutique hotel to meet with some of the managers.

"Mr. Benton, Welcome. Good to see you again," the General Manager stated while shaking his hand. "I am very excited to discuss our next property adventure and location with you. Come on in to my office. What would you like to drink?" He asked while motioning to his assistant to come over and take their orders.

"Corey, always good to see you, bud. I'll have a Blue Moon if you have that on draft." Jim responded back to him.

Christina, Corey's assistant responded, "Sure, absolutely. I'll get that right away Mr. Benton. Would you like something to eat as well?"

Shaking his head and winking in return, "I'm good Hun, thanks."

"Alright, let's get down to business, shall we?" Corey pulled out the blueprint of the next hotel they are looking at building in Europe. They banter back and forth on their ideas, changes and plans before coming up with an opening date.

"I was thinking if we completed the structure of the building in the location we discussed facing the Eiffel Tower, then we could get our guys to complete everything by Winter of next year. That gives us over a year. But only if we get the original space we selected."

While Jim was speaking, Corey pulled out the blueprint of the design of hotel plan B if they must choose another location away from the Eiffel Tower. "Now, if we go with this selection, we already know we could complete it much sooner and it will be within budget. We need to push for the other location however. We will gain much more exposure and business." Jim discussed his thoughts and ideas with Corey, before coming to an agreement on finding ways to win their bid on location A. During their conversation, Christina walked over with two beers and placed them on the desk as they continued chitchatting.

Meanwhile in New York City, the anxiety grew inside Melanie's chest and stomach. Jim still hasn't called or texted her back. She had a feeling in her gut that something wasn't right days ago when the initial calls came through. The hurt and pain she felt was excruciating, and almost unbearable. The only reason she got out of bed today, was to let Buddy out and feed him. The grey and white flannel pajama pants and white t-shirt were still on from the day before. Her hair was going all sorts of directions since it had not been brushed in over a day. Even her breath was terrible since she had no energy to even brush her teeth in over twenty-four hours.

The doorbell rang unexpectedly and buddy barked, as he ran up to the front door. There was no drive in Melanie to even care enough to get out of bed, walk downstairs and answer the door. Even getting up to look through the blinds of their guest room to see who was there wasn't appealing. Buddy continued barking ferociously as the doorbell rang again.

"Melanie! Are you in there? It's me, Kristen." Once Melanie heard Kristen's voice, she got up and rushed downstairs to unlock the door. She gripped Buddy's collar while opening the door to let Kristen in. Buddy's tail was whipping around in circles of excitement when he smelled and recognized her.

"Oh honey, look at you," Kristen remarked while looking at Melanie with sadness in her eyes. Melanie had spoken to her earlier that morning when Kristen was driving to work, since they were both awake. She caught her up on everything from the evening before, and the call from the other day. She really needed a friend and Kristen was her closest friend there. They had known each other for several years and were coworkers back in the day. "Did you eat anything? Let's get you cleaned up, shall we?"

Melanie shook her head, "No, I'm really not hungry at all. I just need a friend right now. Jim will be coming in later today, anyhow."

"I understand. Here, at least drink your favorite coffee I got you from Starbucks." That put a slight smile on Melanie's face. "Well, what are you going to do about Jim now? Are you going to stay with him through this? You know I've had a bad feeling about him since I met you two, and I just want you to be happy. You definitely deserve better than this Melanie."

"I know I do. I'm fully aware. It's hard when you love someone. The thought of him being with another woman is heartbreaking. I don't know if I'll be able to look past this. I need to see him and talk to him face to face to find out more. I don't even know how long this has been going on, or if she was some kind of one-night stand. But this woman told me she loved him. And, this was the same woman I remember him with at that New Year's Eve party where I met him. I mean, that would be way too coincidental if I was wrong, right?"

"Yes. If it's the same woman, then I would question whether something has been going on for a long time, too. If that was the case, he's a disgusting pig. Well, regardless, he is at this point."

Tears strolled down Melanie's face. "I just can't believe he would do this to me. And to us."

Kristen got up and sat right next to Melanie, hugging her and rubbing her back. "I know. No one would ever expect their loved one

Love is a Mysterious Lie

to do such a thing. Especially when making vows to one another. I'm sorry you're going through this."

Melanie cried on Kristen's shoulder. "I wish I could stay longer, but I need to get back to the office. I'll check on you later, okay?" Melanie nodded as she hugged Kristin goodbye.

As Kristen closed the door behind herself, Melanie walked over to the framed wedding picture of her and Jim. She picked it up, and stared into the photo intensely before throwing the frame onto the hardwood floors. The glass cover cracked into numerous pieces, yet staying intact within the frame. The sound of the glass popping startled her, but she left it on the floor anyway.

Sluggishly, she walked back to the door to lock it, then headed back up the stairs to bed. Jim was scheduled to come in to town in a few hours, and she had already planned on picking him up at the airport. Even with this twisted situation, she was still looking forward to seeing him. It didn't change the fact that she still and had always been madly in love with him.

She drifted off to sleep for a short period of time before waking up to her phone buzzing. It was Jim, texting her that he would be arriving a little earlier than expected. He asked if she preferred him getting car service instead.

"That's okay. I can still pick you up." She responded back. Was that really all he's going to say to me after all my messages? He really has the audacity. She reflected on her thoughts for a moment, before getting up to take a shower. The energy to get up and impress him wasn't hard, since she felt this urge to show him what he was losing out on now. Her mind was not made up in any way on what she should do about their marriage.

Normally, she wore jeans and a casual t-shirt. Today, she decided to put on a black, skin tight skirt that was halfway down to her knees, coupled with an off-white blouse that had three-quarter sleeves and black patent leather heels. These were the outfits she used to wear when she went to work, or when Jim and she would go out on dates for cocktails. Putting on this outfit got her feeling nostalgic about the days they went on romantic and sexy dates. Where did all the time go? As she was thinking, she realized she couldn't even remember the last time they went on a date together. Maybe that's because he's been too busy cheating on me.

Chapter 7

It was a cold winter evening in New York city as Jim walked into the party. He went straight over to his buddy Derek and greeted him with their usual handshake. "What's up dude?!" said Jim.

"My dude! How you been? I haven't seen you since you were hooking up with that model sometime last year."

"Oh, Adriana? Yeah, that's still an off and on thing. She's super sexy and a hard one to let go of. It's a lot of fun while I'm traveling on the road."

"Oh, for sure dude. She's gorgeous! She's supposed to be here tonight I think, not sure if you knew." Derek replied.

"You know, she did mention something to me about it, but I got busy with other things and never got back to her."

"Yeah, I hear you. Well bro, go grab yourself a beer or something in the kitchen. I'll catch up with you in a bit. Going to make my rounds," said Derek.

Jim continued walking through the enormous penthouse apartment towards the kitchen to scope out the beverage options. The variety of liquor, beer and wine options were endless. He opted for bourbon on the rocks. As he was pouring his bourbon, Adriana walked into the kitchen with another beautiful blonde on her arm. "Well look who it is!" Adriana shrieked in excitement.

"Hey babe! What's going on?" replied Jim.

"Oh, you know. Living the dream as usual. Ahem, you never texted me back, mister. I wasn't sure if I was going to see you or not. Anyways, this is my friend Melissa." Jim reached out to shake her hand.

"Nice to meet you beautiful," he said before kissing her on the cheek.

Melissa whispered in Adriana's ear, "I now see what you've been talking about with this one. Wow." Adriana pinched Melissa's arm and gave her the hush look.

While Jim was chatting with the ladies, he glanced over Adriana's shoulder and saw Melanie. She was not drop dead gorgeous but had that beautiful girl-next-door look. He thought she was stunning and could not stop staring at her. Through his zoning out, Melanie caught him looking at her and immediately blushed, then looked away in embarrassment. Adriana snapped her fingers at Jim to get his attention.

"What the hell was that for?" Jim bellowed in shock.

"You looked like a lost little puppy for a second there," she said while laughing with Melissa. "What are you looking at anyway?" Before he answered, she turned around and saw Melanie. Melanie was also looking at her, then felt nervous and walked out of her view. Adriana felt flustered that he had the nerve to check out another girl right in front of her face. After turning back towards Jim, she brushed her body against his and whipped her hair around to gain his full attention. When she turned to reach for her drink on the table next to them, she felt Jim's grip on her waist loosen before vanishing; and then he was gone. "Come on Melissa, let's go meet some men. I'm not going to let him bring me down again."

Adriana poured herself and Melissa a glass of Pinot Noir and darted out of the kitchen. Around the corner, was Jim already mingling with Melanie. It appeared they were hitting it off and getting along well. Adriana's blood was boiling in anger and jealousy. She approached the next man that she saw and began flirting intensely with him. Melissa tagged along with her, a little bored since she was now the third wheel. Jim didn't even notice what was going on because he was captured by Melanie. Her hazel eyes were gleaming from the candle flickers. The cute smirks she kept giving him were mesmerizing to him.

Adriana was fuming at this point and had to break up whatever was happening between the two of them. She quickly interrupted their conversation in the moment he was replying "It was my escape. I should be thanking you."

"Thanking her for what darling?" Adriana slyly stated while tossing her hair over her shoulder and squeezing in between them. It was obvious to Melanie that she was trying to mark her territory on Jim.

"Oh, nothing. I was just talking to this lovely lady. Melanie, this is my friend Adriana."

"Nice to meet you," Melanie uneasily replied while shaking her hand.

"Um, yeah, same to you," answered Adriana in disbelief, while rolling her eyes. She felt rather foolish in that moment and walked away from the two of them. As the night continued, she felt more and more rejected by Jim. All her efforts flirting with other men at the party were not doing her any justice. He did not leave Melanie's side the rest of the night. She was hoping to kiss him at midnight and for a little more afterwards; but since that idea seemed shot, she jumped on another handsome fella that was there with his wife, and immediately laid one on him.

"Excuse me!" shrieked the other woman. She slapped Adriana, which knocked her down to the ground. Everyone stopped what they were doing to turn and watch what was happening. Melissa ran over to Adriana to grab her hand and help her up. The tears were streaming down her face. And her mascara turned to goop from the sobbing. The white and black silk dress she was wearing had fallen open and exposed her lack of underwear she should have had on. Her lipstick was smeared across her lips and cheek. Melissa pulled her up and rushed her out the door. Adriana was too drunk to realize what completely happened at that point.

Jim witnessed the entire thing and felt bad for her, but not enough to do anything about it. He was disturbed to watch such a show go down and thought it was rather trashy of her to behave that way. As he turned back to Melanie to continue their conversation, his phone vibrated. He looked down and saw it was Adriana. Instead of opening his phone, he put it back in his pocket and carried on the conversation with Melanie. He felt his phone vibrating every couple of minutes but kept ignoring it.

"I'm sorry about that. We've met a few times before, and I didn't know we both had mutual friends at this party. Anyhow, carry on with what you were saying about your job as an editor. This is quite fascinating to me," Jim said. Melanie was so tipsy that she barely processed the incident that just occurred.

As their conversation continued without barely a hitch, Adriana was a drunken mess stumbling around the city with Melissa. "Girl, what the heck was that? Did you seriously kiss some other woman's husband?" Melissa eagerly asked.

"I don't know what happened exactly. He was hot, and I was jealous of seeing Jim talking to that girl. I wanted to get a rise out of him and that guy was the last one I was talking to before I decided to make a move." She replied while shrugging her shoulders.

Most of what Adriana was saying wasn't making much sense due to how intoxicated she was. Melissa saw her repeatedly text and call Jim on the phone. "You need to stop calling him and leave him alone at this point. I know it hurts, but you deserve better than that. It's pretty clear he views you differently than you see him."

"Well, love makes you do crazy things Melissa, okay? I don't care what you think. He should be with me and he's making a big mistake."

Melissa knew at that point, it was best to keep quiet about the situation. Her drunken mind was going to win every argument because she was relentless. "Should we stop over at another bar?" Melissa inquired.

Adriana requested a taxi through her phone app to pick them up and head downtown. "Goodness gracious, the fare rates are high right now. I should've known since it is New Year's Eve after all. Let's go anyway, are you coming?" Adriana asked.

"Yes. I'd like to meet some men as well," she winked while replying to her. A silver Cadillac pulled up. "Hi, are you Adriana?"

"Yes, that's me," she replied as they got into the taxi driver's car. "Can you take us down to the Sky Lounge please?"

The driver responded, "Yes ma'am. It's about fifteen minutes from here."

The drive felt much longer than it was because Adriana was feeling anxious and impatient. As the car pulled up to the front of the building, the girls hopped out and rushed inside towards the elevator. Neither one thanked the driver, and Adriana paid through the app on her phone as they continued walking in. The girls took the elevator straight up to the rooftop bar. As the elevator doors opened, a crowd of people were surrounding the foyer waiting in line and pushing along to the nearby bar for a cocktail. Several small, dimmed chandeliers hung from the ceiling around the lounge. Black leather couches were in one area of the bar, and a large dance floor in the other. The end of the lounge opened to a large enclosed patio with glass railings overlooking the city.

Love is a Mysterious Lie

Glass window blocks were mounted into the floors of the exterior veranda that lit up in different colors. A variety of men and women almost encompassed the entire surface of the outdoor floors. Melissa pulled Adriana along to the outdoor bar. As they braved the crowd, they both scoped the loads of eye candy surrounding them. A dark-haired man, with blue eyes immediately stopped Adriana by touching the small of her back. "Ladies, can I get you a shot?" He asked, looking them both in the eyes.

Melissa looked at Adriana and laughingly said, "Why of course you can. How about a mind eraser? We could both use that from the evening we've had thus far!" The girls laughed.

"Well, come with me then." He motioned them towards the bar where his friends were and ordered a round of shots.

"Ladies, these are my friends Scott and Mike. And my apologies for being so rude, I forgot to introduce myself to you both. I'm Nick." They all greeted each other after exchanging names. The night went on with various rounds of shots and cocktails, so many that they all lost count at some point. Nick's bill towards the end of the night was roughly $1000 in beverages. He didn't even flinch when he added the tip and signed the bill. Melissa eventually ran off with Scott, and Mike was mingling with some woman during the period of time they were there. "Want to come back to my hotel? I'm staying at the Ritz-Carlton down the road," Adriana asked Nick.

"Absolutely, babe." He drunkenly replied.

They both walked out together hand in hand rushing through the crowd in excitement. Nick hailed a taxi to pick them up outside the building. Shortly after they got into the car, they were making out right before Adriana begun throwing up all over the backseat. "Oh, my goodness, I'm so sorry!" She screeched to the taxi driver and to Nick after realizing she sprayed vomit on him.

"Well, this isn't exactly how I thought my night would be ending," Nick stated. "I'll clean you up in my hotel room," she winked at him. As they departed the taxi, they rushed onto the elevator and upstairs to get him cleaned up. The doorman of the hotel did not seem surprised to see vomit on someone, given the holiday it was.

Once inside her suite, Adriana took a wash cloth and soaked it in water, then cleaned off his shirt. Nick took off his shirt instead, which led her to drop the washcloth to the floor once she saw his ripped abs. Nick got the ball rolling by taking off the rest of his clothes.

"Let me run to the bathroom really quick, please don't stop though," Adriana mentioned while rushing off. She quickly brushed her teeth, then rinsed her mouth out. As well as freshening up her makeup, deodorant and fixing her hair. Then looking down to make sure she shaved. When she walked out of the bathroom, Nick was already on the bed, naked and under the sheets. The rest of the evening turned into a party between the two of them that didn't end until 5 am that same morning.

Chapter 8

Once Melanie finished getting changed, she looked in the mirror at herself. She felt sick to her stomach. Her eyes were still completely swollen from crying all morning and all night. She grabbed a washcloth and ran it under hot water for a few minutes before placing it over her eyes to de-puff them. Melanie thought dressing in a sexy outfit to keep Jim's eyes focused on her body may do the trick to hide the fact that she had been crying. As her eyes slowly calmed down, she applied black eyeliner and mascara, then fixed up her hair. A couple sprays of perfume later and she was out the door.

While driving to the airport, something in her body felt strange. The knot in her stomach still had not gone away since yesterday. Yet, there were still butterflies that filled her stomach when she approached the airport. Her heart was pounding fast, like it normally would before she has a panic attack. There was no sign of Jim yet, so she pulled up to the Delta terminal and waited in the car. Ten minutes had passed when she saw Jim walking out of the airport towards her car. She was even more terrified now after seeing him, and it hit her that this may be the last time she ever picks him up at the airport again. Her heart sank and pounded harder as he came closer to the car.

Jim's heart was also firmly pounding once he was near the car. It surprised him that Melanie hadn't said much else since last night's call. He tried to prepare himself for all the questions he knew that Melanie would throw at him. A part of him felt ashamed for what he has been doing behind her back. Yet, the other part of his brain, enjoyed the thrill Adriana was providing him. It had only been a few hours since they had sex again at the luxury resort they were staying in.

It had been close to a week since he was last home in New York from his work trip in Key West. Lately, he had been flying down there often to get the plans settled on the new hotel they were building overseas. It just so happened that Adriana lived down there, as well, and she normally traveled all over the world for modeling gigs; but this was a slower time for her. It was quite ironic that she knew someone through the grapevine that was throwing a New Year's Eve party in New York years ago, where she flew up to knowing she may see Jim again. She didn't think she would see him too often after their first meeting in a bar up in Chicago, until they bumped into each other a year later in Key West on Duval Street.

That one drunken night turned into years of messy sex and infidelity since he was always dating someone on and off, and then came Melanie. Jim has flown all over the world to meet her for a hot adventure. He traveled often enough that he has been able to arrange some of his trips around her schedule, and he had pulled it off quite effortlessly. It wasn't until recently that their affair turned more serious and intimate between the two of them; at least for her. Adriana has completely fallen head over heels in love with him at that point and there was no turning back. To her surprise, Jim had contemplated leaving Melanie for her because the thrill was addictive. This was the topic of several conversations they had since Adriana has given him ultimatums. Yet, Jim was cleverly able to get himself out of it each time. He always found a way to twist or manipulate things around, where he was no longer at fault.

At this point, Jim was pissed that Adriana completely blew his cover by drunkenly calling Melanie last night. He even wondered if she called Melanie the day prior, too. Now he had to clean up this mess she created; drama does not suit him well. His three sheets to the wind brain last night did not care so much as his sober mind did this morning.

As he inched closer to the car, both his heart and Melanie's were racing simultaneously; with different, yet similar fears. As he came within reach of the passenger door, Melanie got out of the driver's seat and ran around to him. Jim had no idea what was about to happen, and his stomach dropped for a second. She grabbed him and gave him a very endearing hug, squeezing him tighter than ever before. He held her in his arms, "I missed you, baby. And damn, you look sexy as hell!"

Melanie was so overwhelmed, that she couldn't get any words out. Tears were welling up in her eyes. In that moment, she missed him so much that she just needed to be close to him. While they were holding each other, a car honked at them and the security guard walked over. "Excuse me! This area is for picking up passengers only, not hanging around. We have others that need to get in here. Please move your car."

Jim grabbed his suitcase and threw it in the trunk, while Melanie got back into the driver's seat. Neither of them started a conversation, and Jim wanted to avoid one altogether. Once he got into the car, Melanie glanced over at him with sadness in her eyes. She drove away from the airport while glancing over her shoulder to see couples greeting one another around baggage claim. Her heart sank. She briefly reminisced about when she last felt that way for Jim.

Meanwhile, Jim kept checking Melanie out, and he couldn't remember the last time she dressed that way. All he kept thinking about was getting her back to the house and in the bedroom. Yet, he knew he had to distract her beforehand as to avoid any conversation about the incident the evening prior. Jim broke the ice, without acknowledging the elephant in the room on her end. "Babe, want to grab a bite to eat before heading to the house? I've been wanting to check out that new brewery restaurant." Melanie looked over at him in such disappointment, thoroughly stumped by his ignorance. The thought of him in bed with another woman made her stomach feel uneasy.

"Sure," Melanie softly replied. She didn't even know how to talk to Jim anymore. The brewery was several minutes away from the airport and they rode in silence the entire way there, with only soft jazz playing at a low volume. Seconds felt like long, endless minutes.

As Melanie parked the car, Jim hopped out and looked down at his cell phone. Five missed calls from Adriana, and three text messages. "Baby, where are you?" "Have you talked to her?" "Why aren't you responding to me?" Jim put the phone back in his pocket and proceeded up to the restaurant. Melanie was still sitting in the car trying to get her emotions together before being seen in the public eye. Tears were strolling down her face behind her Audrey Hepburn cat eye sunglasses. Jim bought the sunglasses for her last year on a whim, telling her it was just because he loved her.

Now as she thought back, she realized the gift was only because she stumbled across text messages on his phone indicating he may be talking inappropriately to another woman. Was that when our marriage began failing? Her forehead crinkled in confusion. Why did I fall for his lies? Jim told her it was a coworker that met him for a conference in Vegas, and she was going through a divorce, which was why she was talking out of line. She had too much to drink and was very emotional. "He's been lying... this whole entire time, " Melanie muttered to herself, while still sitting in the car.

Jim was waiting outside the front door of the restaurant, back on his phone. Not even paying attention to the fact that Melanie still hadn't stepped out of the car. She went into a zone, got out of the car, took off her sunglasses and smashed them on the ground with her heels. "Take that you lying, cheating, scumbag!" Then shook her head once she realized she had a vision of doing that but couldn't gain the courage to do anything.

She stepped out of the car and walked towards Jim with her head down. Jim, still not realizing his wife was going through such misery, continued text messaging on his cell phone. Once he noticed her approach, he shoved the phone back into his pocket and opened the door for Melanie. Normally, Melanie would walk into a restaurant with pride and her head held high standing by his side. Today, she walked through the door with her head down in disappointment. Her heart was aching, her stomach was turning, and she had no appetite. Jim was too caught up in his thoughts over Adriana's text messages to show any care or affection towards her.

After they were seated, the waiter greeted them both and immediately asked for their drink orders. "What do you have on tap?" Jim asked the male waiter. He went on to list their draft specials and local brewery options. "Get me the Rockaway ESB you have on tap," Jim stated without being a gentleman and allowing Melanie to place her order first.

"I'll have a gin and tonic please." The waiter walked away with the drink orders.

"A gin and tonic, huh? Just like back in the day. I haven't seen you order one of those in a while."

"Well, times call for sentimental moments." Jim didn't understand what she meant by that or how to respond. The thoughts quickly left his head once he was distracted by a football game on the television.

Melanie was thinking over some thoughts in her mind. He is unbelievable. I see no signs of remorse for what happened last night. Of course, he wanted to go to a sports bar and be in a public place where he knows I will not make a scene or confront him about anything. And now he's distracted by the football game. The waiter brought over their drinks and placed them down on the table. "Can I get you two anything to eat as well?" he asked.

"I'll have the salmon Caesar salad, please," Melanie replied.

"And I'll get the bacon cheeseburger with French fries," Jim piggy backed.

"How would you like that cooked sir?"

"Medium."

"I will bring your food out as soon as it's ready," the waiter stated before walking away. Melanie thought it was interesting that Jim had such an appetite since he normally ate light. Then she stressfully thought, did he have sex this morning? It was hard for her to keep this all in without a peep.

"How's Buddy been this week babe?" Jim asked.

"Fine, same old, same old," she responded.

"I bet my boy missed me. He needs a companion, especially when I'm gone."

"Um, he has me. He is not alone Jim. I am the one that takes care of him most of the time. I don't know why you would even say that. He was my dog first anyway," Melanie angrily responded.

"That's not what I meant babe. I was just thinking we should get another dog for him to run around in the yard with. Maybe we should stop by the animal shelter on our way home to check out the other dogs?"

Melanie didn't know how to react to his comments. Was he saying all this to avoid "the talk"? That's exactly what Jim planned. "Sure, we can do that." The rest of their conversation was very basic and surface level. After they wrapped up and Jim signed the receipt, they headed out the door.

"Do you remember how to get to the shelter Jim?" The thought of calling him babe or any affectionate name, made her sick to her stomach since everything was rocky now.

"Yes," he answered as they got back in the car. "Take this road up to Peachtree, turn right and then it's a few miles on the left." They rode to the shelter in more awkward silence, but this time with no music playing. Jim was busy engaging on his cell phone again, and Melanie was wrapped up in her thoughts.

She pulled into the shelter lot and parked the car. They walked into the building separately and not even near one another. It was hard to tell by others they were together from the obvious distance between them. As they walked in, Melanie followed behind Jim towards where the dogs were located. There were so many helpless dogs; a mixture of older ones and puppies. "Should we get a puppy or a dog that's a little older and already trained?" Melanie asked Jim.

"I think a younger pup would be best. Would be good for Buddy." They walked around scoping out all the dogs, then Melanie saw the perfect little yellow Labrador puppy.

"Oh Jim! She's perfect!" Jim knew puppies would do the trick. He walked over to check out the dog, and asked one of the helpers if they could take her out. The lady brought them to a room in the back that was enclosed, and brought the puppy inside.

"This is Bella. She is four months old and is the last of her litter that was found on the side of the road." She placed the puppy down on the ground, and Bella stood there scared and shivering.

"Hi Bella. It's okay sweetie." Melanie walked over to gently pet her. Pretty quickly Bella was wagging her tail in excitement.

Chapter 9

"She's just what we are looking for. We'll take her," Jim said to the lady. His plan seemed to work so far, and maybe she would forget what happened the other day. He wanted to also buy himself more time to find a way out of this mess he got himself into, and to find a way to leave Adriana. The years of infidelity was no longer exciting to him now that he sees how attached she has become. It was supposed to be fun, meaningless sex and it turned more into a relationship. Her constant remarks on leaving his wife, and blowing up his phone, were major turn offs for him.

The lady went to the back office and pulled out all the paperwork for them to sign. She then explained all the details on the puppy, shots and the small payment fee to adopt her. After they completed everything, Melanie picked up Bella and carried her to the car. "Well aren't you just the cutest puppy there ever was!" She said snuggling into Bella's fur coat.

"Looks like we will have to stop by the pet store on our way home to get some things for her," Melanie said while looking at Jim.

"Yes of course, babe."

Bella was bouncing around in the backseat of the car, excited and disordered. They arrived at the pet store, and Jim mentioned, "I'll just stay in the car with Bella if you want to run in and grab a few things?"

"Oh, alright," she replied. As Melanie walked into the pet store, Jim pulled out his cell phone to check his messages from Adriana. "Babe, where are you?? I've been trying to contact you!" "What happened?" "I'm freaking out because I haven't heard much from you since you left my house this morning." The messages were piling in and were stressing him out. Jim texted back, "Sorry babe, we've been busy. I'll catch up with you later." Then put his phone on silent and changed her name in his phone to Steve.

Melanie strolled back to the car with a dog bed in one hand, puppy food in another, and a new collar and leash. As she opened the trunk to put all the stuff in the car she realized she forgot a dog crate.

"Shoot! I didn't get the dog crate for her. Can you go in and grab that Jim?" Jim got out the car and replied, "Sure babe." As he walked inside, Melanie organized the trunk with Bella's new items and hopped into the driver's seat.

Then, she noticed Jim left his cell phone on the passenger's seat. Her anxiety caused pits to form in her stomach at the thought of what could be on that phone. She couldn't help herself but attempt to snoop. She reached for the phone and typed in his password, which had always been their wedding anniversary. But, the passcode didn't work this time. He changed his password, she cried out in her head. She attempted a few other passcodes, but nothing worked. "Well, this sure is concerning now," she stated out loud to herself.

As she put the phone down, Jim approached the car with the dog crate in a large box. "Babe, pop the trunk," he yelled over. Melanie pushed the trunk button to pop it back open, and sat there in a panic. Once he placed the crate in the trunk and got back into the car, he noticed Melanie's face looked different. It took a second before Jim realized his cell phone was sitting there on the seat. Ohhhh shit! He screamed in his mind. But wait, I changed my passcode. There's no way she could have figured it out. Or did she?

"Everything okay babe?" He worryingly asked.

Melanie zoned out, then responded, "Yes, I'm fine." She was so dumbfounded that she didn't know how to approach the topic.

The uneasy feeling in Jim's stomach settled as they drove home, but he could tell something was going on with her. Melanie pulled into the garage, and quickly got out of the car. Then she picked up Bella and walked towards the garage door into the house.

"Can you bring in all of Bella's things please?" She said to Jim. Before he could even answer, she was already inside the house. Buddy was lying in a sun spot on the living room floor when Melanie walked in with Bella in her hand. He jumped up and ran over to her once he saw another dog.

She put Bella down on the ground, and both dogs wagged their tails, sniffing one another. It didn't take long for them to get acquainted and start rough housing with one another. Melanie stood there smiling as she watched the two of them having fun together. Jim walked in the door with all the items in his hands and under his arms. He looked stressed and angry but was abiding right now since he knew Melanie was aware of something going on.

"I'll set up the cage over here around the breakfast nook." Melanie turned towards him and nodded her head in agreement.

She walked over to open the sliding glass doors to let the dogs run around the back yard. After opening the doors, she barged straight towards Jim.

"I can't play this game anymore Jim! You need to tell me what the hell is going on! Have you been cheating on me? Who is the woman that has been calling me? You better fess up right now if you want to salvage anything in this marriage!" She screamed at him.

Been calling? How many times has Adriana contacted her?! Jim was now in panic mode. What lie can he say to get himself out of this? He was stressing out and sweating profusely. "What do you mean? What woman, babe?" He asked, playing dumb.

"Don't play stupid with me Jim! Be honest with me! I am wiser than you may think or realize. I know something is going on. I am completely distraught and heartbroken over all of this. Let me see your phone then."

"There's nothing to see on my phone, I don't know why you need to see it. That's an invasion of my privacy."

"Your privacy? If you have nothing to hide, then you wouldn't be saying that to me. I have a right to ask, and to see what is going on since I know you are not being truthful with me. Especially after these past couple days!" Jim was flustered and in a deep hole that he couldn't find his way out of. He decided to hand over the phone to try and prove to her he had nothing to hide, in the chance she may not look and it was all a bluff.

She took it immediately from his hand, and attempted the passwords.

"Oh, so you changed our anniversary password then, huh? And why is that? What is this new password of yours now Jim?" She angrily asked.

"Yes, I changed it weeks ago for security reasons since I've had the same password for years." Melanie rolled her eyes as he replied with a lying excuse. "The password is now my Dad's birthday." She typed that in, and "voila!" The phone was now unlocked. As she snooped through his texts, she immediately noticed some messages from a guy named Steve, whom she's never heard of. Then reading through them, it all becomes very clear. "Either you're having an affair with a woman, that you changed the name to Steve to, so I wouldn't know, or do you need to tell me that you are gay?! Tell me the truth Jim! I deserve this!" He doesn't know how to possibly get himself out of this mess and chose to fess up.

"No, I'm not gay. Yes, I've been having an affair. I'm terribly sorry, babe."

"Don't call me babe! Is that what you call her? So, it is true?! I just knew it! I love how nonchalant you are acting about all this. As if it's no big deal that you broke our vows. Is it that woman from the party I met you at several years ago??"

"Yes..." Jim frightenedly responded.
Melanie shook her head in disappointment and tears rolled down her face. "I can't believe this. This is unbelievable. My gut knew it. The universe showed me so many signs. I just never thought you would ever do this to me or to us."

"I know babe, uh, Melanie. It wasn't intentional. It just kind of happened for fun before you and I were dating, and it continued. I didn't know how to end it with her."

"This has been going on since we were dating?? Oh, my word... This is too much." Melanie put her hand up to motion Jim to stop speaking. Then grabbed her car keys and purse before storming out of the house.

She had no specific direction of where she was headed. She just needed to get out of the house as soon as possible. During her drive, she broke down crying and was unable to breathe. A small paper bag was in the glove box that she kept in there from previous panic attacks.

She pulled it out and breathed into heavily. Suddenly, she felt extremely nauseous and had to pull over to the side of the road. Puke then spewed out of her mouth onto the shoulder of the highway. The amount that was coming out of her body seemed endless. When the vomit finally stopped, she got back into the car and grabbed some tissues from her purse to wipe her mouth.

Sitting there on the side of the road, with the driver's door still open and looking over her throw-up, she shook her head in disbelief. How did this become my life? What did I do to deserve this? She pondered to herself.

She reached into her purse for her cell phone to reach out to Kristen before realizing she had a missed call and message from a number she didn't recognize. She listened to the voicemail. "Hi Mrs. Benton, this is Margaret from Mrs. Samson's office. We had you and Jim scheduled for an appointment this evening and noticed neither of you showed up. Please give us a call."

"Oh, shit! I completely forgot," she said out loud while shaking her head in distress. She made the appointment a week ago when they were in a much different place. Now, to see they are in this position thanks to his infidelity, she broke down even more. She called the office back and told them a few lies as to why they would not be rescheduling; and apologized for failing to cancel the appointment.

There was too much going on for her to even focus on that, or to really care for that matter. She dialed Kristen's number. "Hey lady, how's it going?" Kristen answered.

"Could be better, actually. It's confirmed that Jim is having an affair. Can I stay with you tonight?"

"Of course! Come over. I'm so sorry you're going through this Melanie."

"Yeah, me too, thanks. I'll be there shortly."

Once she arrived at Kristen's house, she sat in her car for several minutes. Her head was down and her eyes were closed. The tears would not stop falling from her eyes and dropping on her lap. Kristen looked out her window and saw Melanie's car. She rushed out, opened Melanie's door and gave her an embracing hug. The crying turned into sobbing on her friend's shoulder. Kristen helped her get out of the car and held on to carry her into the house. She had never seen her friend like this before. Although she felt Jim was an asshole, she wasn't prepared to see Melanie broken this way. After laying her down on the couch, she firmly stated, "I really hope you leave that douchebag."

"That's so much easier said than done Kristen, you know that. I don't understand what I did to deserve this, I just don't," Melanie cried out, while shaking her head.

"You haven't done a damn thing to deserve this at all. He has been completely taking you and your kind, sweet, huge, loving heart for granted. And you know that! However, you continue standing by his side. I don't understand; but regardless, I support your decisions." She replied to Kristen,

"I know you do, and I appreciate that. I don't know how I'll be able to handle moving past something like this. I never thought he would do this to me. I mean, I know he's a very charming and attractive man, and he has always been a flirt. I just thought he would never jeopardize what we have or break the vows we made together." She continued weeping over all her memories with Jim and how broken it all was now.

"Let me make you some hot tea, run you a bubble bath, and put you to bed. I think you need some rest and relaxation." Kristen got up to boil hot water, then ran a bath for Melanie.

"Thank you for everything. I don't know what I would do without you," she responded, before hugging Kristen tightly.

Chapter 10

Jim decided to take a taxi to the airport instead of having Melanie drop him off, since they were barely on speaking terms. He requested one through an app on his phone which showed the driver was only a few minutes away. Buddy sniffed around his luggage and tucked his tail between his legs while looking up at Jim. He always sensed when Jim was leaving for a while. "Hey Buddy, come here boy." He knelt to pet Buddy. "It's okay Bud, I'll be back in a week. Take care of your Mom. She needs some extra lovin'." Buddy licked his face and wagged his tail. Bella came running around the corner and bumped right into them both. "How did you get out of your crate?!" Jim picked up the puppy, and brought her back over to the crate to lock up.

Ding. Jim looked down at his phone alert to see that the taxi driver had arrived. He grabbed his suitcase, pulled it through the front door and trucked it down the entrance stairway. A black SUV pulled up with bright LED headlights aiming towards the main door. It was still dark out, and quite early in the morning, close to 5:30 a.m. Buddy ran to the front window and shoved his head around the sheer drapes to watch Jim. His tail was wagging, then slowly stopped moving. He watched Jim throw his suitcase in the trunk of the SUV and hop into the car.

Then he was gone and out of sight. Buddy sat there for several minutes still peering outside to see if Jim would return. Many more minutes passed before Buddy laid down, keeping an eye out for him.

The taxicab pulled up to the Delta terminal. "Safe travels to you, Mr. Benton. I'll see you next week." He then drove away, as Jim walked through the automated double doors into the airport. Since he was a frequent traveler, he skipped all the lines with his status. The airport was rather slow for a Monday morning, which was quite unusual. Jim made it through security in a breeze, then walked to Starbucks to get his regular coffee. It was the same barista he normally saw each time he flew out on Monday mornings.

"Good Morning Mr. Benton. A Grande pikes place medium roast with a splash of whole milk for you?" Christina, the barista greeted.

"You got it. Thanks Hun." Jim was always so friendly and flirtatious with the baristas in the coffee shop. They soaked it all in every time. He was a very handsome and charming man. Dressed in his business suit every time he flew; the ladies were always pining over him. The barista blushed while making his coffee. She wrote his name on the cup with a heart over the "I". Jim picked up his coffee and gave her a wink before walking away.

Melanie slowly woke up to Bella's whining, close to 7:00 a.m. She came back last night, but she and Jim were still barely speaking. While lying in bed, her body felt stiff as she stretched out across the entire mattress. Slowly, she meandered out of bed and did a few yoga poses to loosen up her muscles. Suddenly, she felt a rush of sickness in her stomach and ran to the restroom. All the stress was putting a large toll on her and her body. She hadn't been feeling like herself in weeks. Kristen sent her a couple text messages to check-in and see how she was holding up.

Once she realized how many times Kristen had messaged her and that she was showing concern, her doorbell rang. A sheer, silk robe was laying across the chaise lounge in the bedroom that she threw on before heading down the stairs. Through the side windows around the front door, she could see Kristen standing there. As Melanie opened the door, Kristen nearly fell on her out of relief.

"You're okay, phew! I was so concerned since you didn't return my calls last night or messages this morning. I wasn't sure if he did something to you!"

"Jim isn't like that, you know that. But I'm sorry I worried you like that. I have been physically sick from this and just haven't been myself. Technically, I wasn't even myself prior to this incident."

"I know, I can tell you seem much more different than usual."

"Do you want to come in?"

"Thought you'd never ask." Kristen entered the house and made herself at home, heading straight to the kitchen.

"Did you make any coffee?"

"Not yet, but I can brew some now." Melanie pulled out the mason jar filled with coffee grounds and a paper filter. As she was getting it all together, she ran to the bathroom to throw up again.

Kristen rushed over to the bathroom door and knocked on it. "My goodness Melanie, are you okay?? Wow, I didn't realize you were literally sick over all this."

A couple minutes later, Melanie walked out after rinsing her mouth. "Yes, this has been eating me up inside, I guess."

"You don't think you're pregnant, do you?" Kristen asked in wonder.

"I think it's just the stress of everything. My body is very sensitive when I have anxiety and stress."

"I understand. I've just never seen you this way before, even when you've been really stressed. Why don't we get a test at the store just to be sure?"

Melanie sighed. "I'm not pregnant Kristen, but fine, it'll at least get me out of the house for a little bit." She finished brewing the coffee, then took out a couple to-go cups and lids. The steam from the coffee swiveled up into the air after being poured into the Styrofoam cups. They both added cream and sugar, stirred them up, then took a sip. Simultaneously, burning their tongues as they tasted it.

"Holy shit!" Kristen screeched. Both ladies looked at each other and laughed at their foolishness.

When the moment passed, they took their coffee and headed into the garage. Melanie locked up the house before they get into her car and drove to the pharmacy. To relax her nerves, she blasted "Girls Just Wanna Have Fun" on the radio as they jammed out on their way there. After parking the car, they walked into the store hand in hand.

"It's going to be okay. If you are, you are. You won't be doing this alone, I promise." Melanie smiled at Kristen and squeezed her hand in appreciation. They walked in and went straight to the aisle with the pregnancy tests.

There were so many options to choose from that it became very taxing for Melanie. Her friend could see that she was stressed out by the overwhelming number of options.

"Why don't we just choose one that is cheap and generic? Let's not get carried away. Here, this one comes with three tests and is on sale. That way at least you'll be sure." She picked up the box, grabbed Melanie's hand and dragged her towards the register. Kristen pulled out her wallet and paid for them before Melanie could get hers out in time.

"You didn't have to do that! Thank you."

"It's my pleasure. It's clear you're frazzled. Now let's get you home and figure this out."

They got back in the car and drove back to the house. Melanie beelined straight to the bathroom with the three pregnancy tests in hand as soon as they walked in the door. She stayed in there for several minutes. As she walked out of the bathroom, she said to Kristen, "I can't look. You'll have to check and tell me."

Kristen walked over to her, gave her a half smile, and then walked into the bathroom to check the results. "Alright, here we go." She looks down at all three-laying side by side. Two show she was pregnant, one does not. "Well... I don't know any other way of telling you this, but you are pregnant," she said while showing Melanie the results.

Melanie took the sticks out of Kristen's hands and stared at them blankly. "No, no, no! This can't be right! The timing isn't right at all and this is supposed to be an exciting time." Furious and distraught, she took the pregnancy tests and threw them in the trash.

"This isn't really happening, is it? Please tell me this is a dream?"

Kristen walked over to her and gave her a hug. "I know this is hard, and the timing isn't right, but maybe this could be a blessing? This is a miracle you got pregnant in the first place. Weren't you told it would be hard from the issues you had with your ovaries?"

"Yes..." Melanie responded.

"Well, then this is a dream! I know it's not the ideal situation, let's not focus on that right now."

"I need to think all this through, and how, when or if I'm going to tell Jim. I don't know if I should do this alone. There's so much to figure out." Melanie was pacing through the kitchen to the living room and back, with thoughts spinning in her head.

Jim arrived in Chicago and took a cab straight to one of the hotels where he had a business meeting. When he arrived, he retrieved his luggage and went inside towards the front desk. "Good afternoon, Mr. Benton. How were your travels?" The front desk agent inquired.

"Great, thanks sugar. Listen, could you hold onto my luggage for right now while I jump into this meeting? Also, could you consider changing my reservation for just tonight instead of the week and waiving the fee?"

"Yes, absolutely Mr. Benton." The agent took his luggage and stored it in the closest near the front desk. Jim decided to change his reservation to one night, and get back home to Melanie. During his flight here, he did a lot of thinking. Their marriage was falling apart, and he was the only one to blame for his infidelity. He wanted to come back early and surprise her, in hopes of mending things and making them right for a change.

After his meeting ended, he called the airline in the hotel lobby and changed his flight to the following morning.

"Mr. Benton." The front desk agent said, "I was able to switch your reservation to just one night tonight with no fee due to your status, and we have your room ready if you would like to check-in?" Jim nodded his head as he walked towards her. "You'll be on the sixth floor in room 610, Mr. Benton. Let us know if there is anything we can do to better accommodate you during your stay." Without realizing his rudeness, he snatched the key card out of her hand, and picked up his luggage before rushing off to his room.

Per the normal, they upgraded him to a suite since he was a frequent traveler with a platinum status and he stayed with them rather often. Once he dragged his luggage in, he took out his laptop and immediately sent a few e-mails postponing some meetings and rescheduling them for later in the week. He then jumped on a few websites to have flowers delivered to Melanie and paid the extra fees for them to arrive today. Next, he looked up a few other things for gift ideas and a possible little getaway for the two of them.

Meanwhile in New York, Melanie headed into the city to have dinner with Kristen and to get out of the house after the surprising news from earlier. They went to a quaint little Italian restaurant that served the best spaghetti and meatballs in the city. Once they finished dining, they took the train back to Melanie's house. When they arrived, Melanie saw the flowers at the front door. "What the?!" She got out of the car to check whom they were from, and saw a sweet poem from Jim.

"Do you think he knows?? That can't be possible, right?"

"Of course not, there's no way he knows. He's probably trying to mend what he broke." They were a mixture of sunflowers, lilies and roses, shades of yellow, white, pink, purple and blue pops of color in a beautiful arrangement.

The following morning, Melanie woke up sick again and needed to get fresh air almost instantly. She took the dogs out on a nice nature walk, down to one of the coffee shops. While she was out of the house, Jim arrived back home to surprise her. He was confused to see the house empty, even without the dogs. As he walked around looking for Melanie, he saw an empty pink and white box on the kitchen counter. When he walked closer to it, he noticed it was a box of pregnancy tests. Shocked and nervous, he ran into the first bathroom downstairs to see if the tests were in the trash. The first thing he saw were the positive tests and he went into a full-blown panic. "Holy shit!" He yelled out. He couldn't decide if he felt more anxious or excited.

After his moment of fear, he knew exactly what he needed to do and where his priorities stood. Jim texted Adriana that he no longer wanted to continue their affair, or to see or speak to her again without any further explanation. When Adriana saw the message, her heart sank in devastation. She called Jim, repeatedly, but he kept sending all her calls to voicemail and ignored all her texts. She fell into panic mode and was unable to handle the anxiety. This triggered her emotions back to the feelings she had when he "chose" Melanie over her at the New Year's Eve party years ago.

Chapter 11

Adriana continued contacting Jim relentlessly, by text and phone calls, with no success. It seemed at this point, he may have blocked her. At least that is what she assumed since every time she tried calling him, it went straight to voicemail. She shook her head in disbelief that he had chosen to do this, but she refused to give up. As the weeks passed, she tried living her life like she normally would and attempted moving on, but she just couldn't get over him. Her mind was playing tricks and games on her, and she felt like she was going crazy. It was early in the morning, on a Saturday, as she woke up and jumped on her computer. She searched flights and hotels to New York City. "If he won't give me any closure, then I'll be sure to get it myself," she said out loud to herself.

She had the next couple of weeks off in between modeling gigs to do whatever she pleased. And she was feeling quite spontaneous to do something a little outrageous. She found a flight out later that day, and even a hotel right outside the city; then quickly booked them both. Time was of the essence, as she needed to be at the airport in a few hours. After she jumped off the computer, she rushed to her closet and pulled out her large Louis Vuitton luggage bag. She threw all sorts of outfits inside the empty suitcase. After she packed an assortment of fashions, she hauled her bag towards the front door. "Might as well head towards the airport, and a grab a bite to eat on the way there. I can't believe I'm actually doing this!" She muttered to herself.

As she arrived at the airport after stopping for lunch, she parked her car in the long-term garage, since she would be out of town for a few days. After she entered the airport with her luggage, she walked straight to pre-check with the electronic ticket on her phone. Then went through security, and headed to the bar near her gate. A drink was necessary for this crazy plan she had made. "I'll take a bloody Mary please," she said to the bartender. The bartender quickly prepared her drink while several others were telling him their orders.

"Here you go ma'am, would you like to keep the tab open?" The bartender asked Adriana.

She looked down at her watch to see how much time she had left before her flight. "Sure, go ahead. I have about an hour until my flight takes off." Several drinks were squeezed in that short time frame. She closed out her tab and stumbled over to her gate. When she got in line to board the plane, the other passengers stepped away from her due to the overwhelming smell of alcohol seeping out of her pores. Once she made it on the plane, she put on her head phones and immediately fell asleep during the entire flight.

"Ladies and gentlemen, please fasten your seatbelts as we begin our decent into New York." Adriana woke up startled, without even realizing her music had stopped since it finished the playlist. Drool dripped down her chin and onto her white blouse. O.M.G. She thought to herself. Embarrassingly, she promptly wiped her chin with her hand to hide the evidence of saliva.

After the plane landed, and everyone departed with their bags in hand, she went straight outside to hail a taxi. A black and yellow checkered car pulled up, and a second later the trunk opened for her. The driver got out of the car and grabbed her luggage. "Can you take me to this hotel in Brooklyn please?" She said, pointing to her phone showing the address.

"Yes ma'am," he answered with a thick Russian accent.

During the drive to the hotel, Adriana Googled the distance again to Jim's house. He was supposed to be traveling out of town for the next several days, if his schedule hadn't changed from what he mentioned in their last conversation together. According to Google Maps, her hotel was only 3 miles from Jim and Melanie's house. Walking was out of the question, but perhaps she could take a bike down there or a cab if necessary. As the driver pulled up to the hotel, she paid him and grabbed her luggage out of the trunk before he had a chance to assist. The automatic lobby doors opened as she approached them and walked in.

"Good Afternoon. Are you checking-in?" The front desk agent greeted.

"Yes. And, I was wondering, do you all have bikes to rent out here or are there any places nearby that rent them out?"

"As a matter of fact, we do have bike rentals here. Would you like me to reserve one for you?"

"Yes, I would like it for my entire stay please. Does it have a basket?"

"Okay, no problem at all. Some of them do have baskets and others do not. I can reserve one for you with a basket if you prefer."

"Great, thank you." The agent completed her check-in and handed over the hotel room key, along with the bike lock code for the rental.

After she was settled into her room, she researched the neighborhood and trails to get over to Jim's house. It was hard for her to believe she was not only here, but also going through with this. She ordered room service for dinner, and called it a night early so she could get started bright and early the next morning.

The alarm clock next to the bed beeped loudly the following morning, on the dot at 7:00. Adriana rolled over to turn it off, hopped out of bed and went straight into the shower. After a quick rinse, she put on her designer athletic apparel, threw her hair up in a ponytail then grabbed her purse with her phone and the bike code.

After she went outside and located her bike rental, she tossed her things in the front basket and opened the GPS on her phone to find the nearest coffee shop. A bagel and coffee shop were the closest in distance, so she hopped on the bike and headed that way. When she approached the café, she locked up the bike and went inside to grab a quick cup of joe and a pastry. Her heart was pounding harder and faster at the thought of her next adventure on the bike. The coffee went right down like water before she darted out of there on the bike. She rode through several neighborhoods, taking in the sights of the beautiful brick and stone homes before finally arriving at Jim's house. She had never seen his house before and seeing it for the first time was giving her anxiety. Nausea grew in her stomach as she rode towards the house.

She leaned the bike up against a tree at the house next door, then ran around the side of their house. It wasn't obvious whether Melanie was home or not since there were no cars in the driveway. As she snuck around the house, ducking in and out of the bushes and trees, she peeked in the windows to see what was going on. There was no one around in every window she glanced in. Suddenly, Buddy saw Adriana in the window and ran up. Her heart was racing rapidly while she bent down even lower, and ran further back to another bush to hide behind.

"Buddy, what are you yapping at?" Melanie yelled across the room.

She walked up to the window to look out, but didn't see anything. "Are you barking at a squirrel again?" She asked, knowing he couldn't respond. Then, she let him and Bella out in the backyard to run around. Adriana saw the dogs running around in the yard and that Melanie had left the backdoor cracked open. The dogs ran off into the distance of the yard, which gave her an opportunity to dart inside the house. She took the chance, jumped the fence and sprinted inside the house. Melanie was upstairs but instantly heard the patio door close downstairs.

"Hello?" She called out. "Is someone there?" As she walked back down the stairs, Adriana sprung around the corner with a large knife in one hand and holding a pregnancy test in the other.

She pointed the knife towards Melanie, "You're pregnant? Are you kidding me?? Tell me you're not pregnant and this is a joke!"

Melanie was shaking and responded with a trembling voice, "Who are you? Adriana? The woman that's been having an affair with my husband?!"

"I asked if you were PREGNANT!" Adriana screamed and her eyes became bloodshot. Melanie, now terrified for her life, ran up the stairs to find a phone and call 911. Adriana chased after her and grabbed her feet before Melanie made it all the way up the stairs, and she fall hard onto her stomach.

She began crying uncontrollably, "Please, don't hurt me! What do you want from me? I don't understand!" Adriana held the knife up to her neck, in anticipation of slicing it open. "ARE YOU PREGNANT?" She screamed one last time. Her eyes eagerly stared into Melanie's, with a look of danger.

"Yes…" Melanie quivered.

Adriana lost focus, then suddenly broke down. "That bastard left me because you are pregnant! He never even told me, he just ended it out of the blue!" As Melanie could see Adriana was losing control, she fought her way out of the grip she had on her with the knife. She quickly stood up, but it was too late before Adriana gained focus again and shoved her down the stairs. Her body flailed down the stairs, rolling intensely and finally landing brutally onto the ground. It was hard to tell if she was alive. Blood gushed out of her nose and formed a puddle on the hardwood floor beneath her head.

"Ohhhh shit! What did I do?!" Adriana cried out. She took the knife with her as she ran down the stairs, then climbed over Melanie's body before darting back out to her bike. The dogs ran up to the patio door growling and barking violently as they saw Adriana sprint off.

After she shoved the knife in her backpack, she took off to the nearest gas station. She didn't want anyone to track her by using her cell phone, so she called 911 from the payphone.

"911, what's your emergency?"

"There's an injured woman at 910 Gardenia Avenue," Adriana firmly stated, then hung up the phone. A large dumpster was around the corner of the gas station that she rode over to, and she threw the knife into it. She quickly hopped back onto the bike and rode back to the hotel.

An emergency vehicle and police cars showed up at Melanie's house. The officers pounded on the door, but no one answered. The dogs were still barking uncontrollably from the backyard. The officers tried opening the door but it was locked. One of the paramedics ran around to the backyard, and through the back door to find Melanie lying in her blood on the floor. "Come around back!" He yelled through his two-way radio to the others. Two other paramedics and two police officers ran around back to assist him. One of the paramedics opened the front door to bring in the gurney. They all carefully picked her up and placed her body on the gurney. Another paramedic then hooked her up to an IV.

After they rushed Melanie to the hospital, they performed an emergency procedure on her broken ribs and one broken arm. Jim was contacted by one of the Doctor's at the hospital, but he was in Chicago and couldn't make it over there until the following morning. He informed the Doctor that she was pregnant, and to call him as soon as they had the status on her and the baby. The Doctors' continued running tests and checking on Melanie, until she was finally resting on the hospital bed in the wee hours of the morning.

Jim arrived in the city that following morning on a red eye, and went straight to the hospital. He was very confused as to what happened and how she got here in the first place. The Doctors' thought she may have fallen down the stairs since it looked that way to the paramedics. However, it didn't explain the lady that called 911. After several hours, sitting by Melanie's side, she finally woke up dazed and puzzled. "Wait, what? That wasn't a dream I had?! Oh, my goodness. Jim, please tell me the baby is okay?" She asked, already crying.

"Our baby is surprisingly fine after that hard fall you seemed to have. That little one is going to be a tough kid."

"Wait, you knew I was pregnant? I just realized I never even told you…" Melanie inquired, not only confused from the accident but also how he found out.

"Well, when I came home early that one day to surprise you, I saw the boxes of pregnancy tests, and rummaged through the trash to see the results. I didn't know how to ask you, so I kept it to myself, given the sensitive topic we have already been dealing with. I was giving it time to see when you were ready to tell me. And, I also didn't know how to tell you that after I saw that, I made sure Adriana knew it was over between us. I feel so guilty for all of this and I know it's all my fault. Honey, I can't apologize enough for all the stress and anxiety I have put you through. I can't even believe you are still with me, and that now we are going to have a baby," Jim confessed.

Melanie smiled in astonishment. "I can't believe our baby is okay. I can't even believe I am. I thought she killed us both."

"Hold on, she? Who are you talking about Melanie?"

"Oh, Jim! I was so scared and didn't know what was happening. Adriana showed up with a knife in our kitchen..." She went on to explain the whole story and Jim's blood quickly boiled. He felt even worse knowing that Adriana acted out due to the fact he disappeared on her. As soon as she finished telling him the story, Jim got on the phone to call the police and press charges, in addition to filing a restraining order against Adriana.

Chapter 12

When Adriana was little, she grew up in a very toxic and unhealthy environment. Her Dad was a drug addict, and her Mom had several different personality disorders. They were both toxic to each other, let alone to their children, as well. Adriana also grew up with one older brother and one younger sister. During her pre-teen years, she went through a period where she felt invisible in the family, as if she was the step child. She was always given the most chores; and if she misbehaved in any way or did not follow through with the tasks she was given, then she would be disciplined by being spanked, grounded or sent to her room in silence.

Over the years, it got so out of control, that she didn't even know how to follow through with anything; since she always seemed to be a disappointment to her family. She rarely felt any sort of love by them, and at times, she felt like a slave. On numerous occasions, she tried running away, mostly for attention to see if they cared that she was gone. They never did, and they never went looking for her.

It caused her to sink into further depression as a young child. There were times she even went to extremes to gain attention from her family, just to see some sort of love from them. One day, she tried disappearing somewhere around the house for several hours, to see if anyone noticed she was gone. She hid in the guest room closet and laid in the fetal position for a long period of time. No one went searching for her again. So, she cried and cried like that for hours over the fact that no one was concerned about her whereabouts.

As time went on and she grew into her teenage years, the feelings inside her became more intense. The lack of love was an excruciating emotion for her. She went through periods of wanting to kill herself, but she never had the courage to do it. At one point, she grabbed a knife in front of her family and threatened to slit her wrists, all for a little bit of attention and love. Adriana couldn't tell at the time whether anyone would have been affected or not if she killed herself; but regardless, the attempts never got her anywhere.

At another point, she grabbed a heavy book and banged it against her head several times in front of them, saying she wanted to die and that she hated herself. Nothing came of that either. Adriana had a hard time controlling those emotional outbursts of not wanting to live, and of making it apparent to her parents. Sadly, nothing she did gave her the affection she was seeking from them. Some days, she felt they would be better off without her since she seemed to always be a burden.

During her middle school and high school years, her father would come home high on some type of drug and his fuse shortened each time he was drugged up. When those moments occurred, so did the screaming matches amongst the family. At times it would either end by someone storming off angrily while slamming doors, or the kids would get a beating for something they did "wrong". Anger and physical abuse were common ways they would handle several issues or problems.

At the time, her parents felt that would resolve the problem at hand. Perhaps from the way their parents acted toward them as children; it was hard to understand why they behaved that way. However, their actions caused Adriana to become more and more dejected, that she became a codependent young woman with other people. And all the relationships she was involved in were toxic. That was all she knew growing up and it was what she was familiar with, so it wasn't uncomfortable for her on some strange level. She was somehow drawn to those people without realizing it, or she would unknowingly attract them. Being given love would be foreign to her.

Whenever an issue would arise where she was not at fault in the household, she would be to blame for the bad behavior and would get in trouble for their actions. Then she was forced to apologize for their ruthless way of handling things. It made sense as to why she grew up thinking she was responsible for other people's feelings and actions. Those deeds became so ingrained in her that if someone was ever angry with her, she would take fault and apologize for making them upset. Adriana did not realize at the time that no one can control another person's feelings or outbursts; because as a child it did not work that way.

When things didn't seem right to her, she knew better than to speak up. It was always in her best interest to play by their rules to find any sort of peace and harmony at home. A lot of her days were spent in her room, listening to music, or journaling on her bed.

Although there were a lot of difficult times, there were surprisingly some fond memories with her family as well; such as, pizza nights they would have together while watching movies. She also loved the family dinners they shared. However, as soon as dinner was over, it became a fight as to who was to clear the table and assist with the dirty dishes. Normally, it was Adriana or her sister since her parents were old fashioned. There was a lot that was put on the girls in the family to do most the chores and housework; but most of it was sent her way and not her sister's. This was another reason she felt like the stepchild in the family.

The holidays were also something she had loving memories of. Close to Halloween, they would always pick out a pumpkin together and carve it with silly faces. Christmas was spent with several of their extended family members that lived nearby. Her Aunt Alberta would usually host their Christmas parties, and gift opening gatherings. She will always cherish the good times she could remember. Unfortunately, the verbal and physical abuse she lived in for all those years overtook a lot of that. The bad outweighed the good most of the time, but she tried to grab a hold of the fun times they had and would stay in fantasy land as often as she could.

Years after high school, Adriana did some soul searching for who she was and for someone to love her. It was something she looked for in every relationship. Although, it was very hard for her to distinguish toxic and unhealthy behaviors in several people; since being around those types made her feel at "home" and "safe". Several of her relationships ranged from dating alcoholics, those with drug addictions, in major need of anger management, verbally and physically abusive, and those that criticized her non-stop.

The criticism wasn't something out of the ordinary to her. She was told in more ways than one the disappointment her family saw in her, so she often felt she was never good enough; no matter how hard she tried to follow the rules. It was not that she was necessarily used to this feeling of being disapproved by them, or anyone for that matter, but she didn't know any different. When she would meet people that were nice and treated her well, she wasn't sure how to handle being with someone like that. It always felt that something was wrong or missing, because drama was not attached to the relationship. It was a sick, twisted game she became so wrapped up in that she didn't know how to detach from it all. Hence, why she got caught up in dating Jim, knowing fully well about Melanie, and later why she continued the affair after their marriage. That was one of the reasons at least.

In her defense, Jim was a Narcissist to a T and a master manipulator. He was very clever at twisting words and stories around so she would second guess her own thoughts. The amount of power he had over her psyche was quite insane. After the last crazy encounter she pulled, showing up at Jim and Melanie's house, it hit her hard like a ton of bricks. This wasn't who she wanted to be anymore, or how she wanted to live her life. This unsuccessful situation she got herself into was the cherry on top, giving her the wake-up call she needed. It was time to finally change her life, and her direction, cut out toxic people from her life and other harmful behaviors. However, it was now up to her on which path she wanted to take.

Although her childhood was many moons ago, a lot those memories felt like yesterday. Sometimes, it felt like it wasn't her life. Her mother also continued living vicariously through her. Modeling wasn't something she wanted to do growing up. Yet her Mom knew it would be an easy way to earn money for herself, and to use her daughter to get what she wanted. It was time for Adriana to regain control of her life.

Chapter 13

Adriana woke up sick and was over the toilet early in the morning. The anxiety and stress were affecting her in more ways than one. She hadn't heard from Jim in several months at this point. She was barely eating, and would vomit any fluids she drank.

It had been a week since she was supposed to have her period. She was starting to wonder if all the morning sickness was something more than the tension. During those thoughts, she jumped into her car and headed to the drug store. As she rushed through the double doors, she beelined straight to the aisle for pregnancy tests. Then picked out a few different ones to be sure the results were clear.

While driving back home, the clouds began rolling in fast. Massive drops of rain splattered on her windshield as she pulled into the driveway. While turning off the car engine, she sat there in silence watching the drops glide down her windshield. Tears welled up in her eyes. "What if I'm pregnant?" She softly said to herself. She snatched the pharmacy bag before she could think any further, then ran inside, using the hood of her jacket to shield her head from the rain.

Her bungalow was very quaint and small, overlooking the water from the back patio. When she walked through the door, she threw her keys down and darted to the bathroom. All the pregnancy boxes were unpackaged in a matter of seconds. Plastic and instruction manuals were falling on the floor and were spread out on her vanity. After following the instructions on three separate wands, she placed them on the vanity and stared intently. Her heart beat faster and faster. The anxiety grew inside her and the butterflies multiplied.

Seconds felt like hours for her. She paced down the hallway and returned to see the results. All three said she was pregnant, in three different ways. "No! This can't be happening!" She shrieked. Adriana reached for her cell phone in her back pocket, and pulled it out to dial her best friend's number.

"Hey you! What's going on?" Stacy greeted. Weeping sounds echo on the other end of the phone.

"Hey..." She quietly replied.

"What's wrong??" asked Stacy.

"Stacy...," then silence for several seconds. "I'm pregnant."

"What! Are you serious?! I thought you all were using protection??"

"Yes, I'm dead serious. I took three tests, and they all say positive. We were using it for a period of time, but Jim liked the feeling more when we didn't, so we stopped paying attention at some point. That sure back fired on me. What am I going to do??" Adriana continued sobbing over the phone. "I don't think I can do this. Jim has already left me. And I haven't even told you what I did weeks ago..."

"Okay, let's slow down for a minute. There's no guarantee what he will do when he finds out. But first off, do you even want to go through with the pregnancy? There are more options than one, Adriana. And is he still married to that woman? I forgot her name. What did you do weeks ago?"

"Yes, he's still married. After what I did, he's never coming back. I don't think I can handle this on my own. He won't leave her for me because I'm pregnant, since I discovered she's pregnant too. Although, I don't know if that's still the case now..."

"Whoa! Why do you say that? Okay, let's start with baby steps right now. Pun intended," teased Stacy. Adriana chuckled on the other end of the line, then the smile faded off.

"How about we go to the doctor together to verify you're actually pregnant?"

"I suppose that's a good idea. I'll set up an appointment for this week and let you know the details to meet me if you can. I really appreciate you doing this with me. I'll explain everything to you later."

"Of course. That's what friends are for. I'll chat with you soon." Stacy hung up the phone. Adriana opened her French doors to the patio and laid down on the couch. While watching and listening to the rain settle in the ocean. She laid her head on her hands, overthinking all the possibilities as to where this may lead. A few minutes later, she dozed off into dreamland.

As the sun set, a sun beam shined through the horizon onto her face. Her eyes slowly opened back up. As she sat up, she looked around the patio, dazed and confused after waking up from the deep sleep. It then hit her that the pregnancy was not a dream; it was her reality now. Gradually, she peeled herself off the couch and dragged her feet to her bathroom. One by one, she took off her clothes and jewelry, turned on the hot water in the shower and climbed in. The water dribbled out, spraying the top of her head once she stepped in. Water splashed onto the glass walls and the steam from the heat fogged up the shower door.

Adriana's head dropped down under the shower head, and the water crashed around each side of her ears. She stared blankly down to the stoned tiles under her feet, watching the water pool around her toes. The motivation to even wash her hair in that moment had dissipated. She closed her eyes, and continued weeping. Several minutes passed as she remained standing in the shower, doing nothing but cry. She turned off the water, grabbed her towel and walked to the kitchen. Then she opened each drawer ferociously searching for a bottle opener until she finally found one.

The wine was hanging upside down on a rack attached to the wall. She reached for the bottle of Merlot, and used the corkscrew to pop out the cork. The wine glasses were sparkling at her through the window cabinets when she reached in and grabbed one. After she poured the wine, she put the bottle back down on the counter. In that moment, before taking her first sip, it hit her when she realized she can't drink; she was pregnant. Drinking was normally her crutch during stressful times. Now that wasn't possible. "Well this is just great," she babbled to herself while letting out a loud sigh of frustration.

Adriana took the bottle of wine and carried it over to the sink in the island, then poured it down the drain. As the wine was emptying out, she mumbled "C'est la vie." Red stains splashed all over the stainless-steel sink and onto the white granite countertop. After she tossed the bottle into her recycling bin, she reached for a sponge and wiped down the counter and sink. Her towel fell to the floor and suddenly she heard, "ding-dong."

She jumped up startled, then reached for her towel and quickly wrapped it around her body. And the wet, blotchy sponge fell onto the tiled floor. As she peeked around the corner towards the door, and caught a glimpse through the patterned glass window on the door, she saw what looked like a man dressed in dark attire. "Jim?" She faintly called out. Her heart was pounding faster and faster at the thought that he was at the door. Without caring that her hair was sopping wet still, and being covered in only a towel, she darted towards the door. The door lock was jammed, and she had to fiddle with it until it finally opened. A handsome police officer was standing there, holding papers.

"Good day ma'am. Are you Adriana Santos?" The officer asked.

"Yes. What is going on? Is someone dead that I know? What is happening?!" She fearfully responded.

The officer looked at the panic on her face. "No ma'am. No one is dead. Unfortunately, you have been served." He handed over the papers, then walked away leaving Adriana in confusion. She walked back inside and slammed the door shut. She was too anxious to move any further, and started sifting through the papers, reading intently. Jim and Melanie had filed a restraining order on her.

"Those assholes!" She shrieked. "I cannot believe he is doing this to me! He has some nerve," she angrily said to her empty house. "I mean, to break up with me and now send me these damn papers! I know I did something stupid with your... Wife, ugh. But still, like seriously Jim?! I don't deserve this! I even stopped trying to contact you over a week ago!" She threw the documents down to the ground and stormed to her bedroom. She tossed the towel on the bed and put on her dirty skinny jeans she had lying on the floor. Then threw on a neon pink sports bra and white tank top. After dressing herself, she reached into her closet and snatched her white baseball cap, and flipped it onto her head.

Adriana dashed down the hall back towards the front door, picked up her car keys and sprinted through the door. The door loudly slammed shut while she hopped into the car. As she put her seatbelt on she looked out the window to the glistened grass from the rain storm earlier; then realized she forgot to lock the front door. "Oh well, whatever. Take whatever you want thieves!" She shouted to herself, already pointing fingers at Melanie and Jim with the assumptions in her head. Speed limit signs rapidly passed her by. Carrie Underwood's song Before He Cheats was blaring through the speakers of her Mercedes Benz. "Oh, the irony. He already cheated!" She yelled.

People walking their dogs and pushing baby strollers all stopped to stare at her car zoom by. The music was playing so loudly and disturbed everyone outside on the streets. The sun was shining its last beam into the sky before it finally set. Adriana parked off a side road near Duval Street, which was crowded with party goers. She locked her door and followed the noise of the streets to the bars. The popular street was filled with a mixture of bars, restaurants and shops. People were screaming obscenities as she passed them by. The stench around her reeked of old stale alcohol. While walking down the path, she could see a crowd of people she knew in the distance. They were always her go-to crew when she wanted to party and let loose. Basically, to forget whatever moment she was in.

"Adriana! Where have you been girl?! It's been a long time since we've seen you here!" A man in his thirties howled over.

"Hi babe! I know, it's been a long time. I've had a lot going on, but I'm here to have some fun now! I'm so glad I ran into you all. What's on the agenda tonight?"

"Sloppy Joe's first, and we will play it by ear from there."

"Sounds like a plan," she responded. Looking around, Adriana noticed she didn't recognize half the people in the group anymore. How long has it been since I partied with these people? She didn't realize how much time Jim really took away from her social life, although, it wasn't a bad thing since it kept her out of the drug scene this long. In that moment, she didn't care one way or another. Her head was not in a good place and she wanted to drink away her sorrows. I wouldn't be a good Mom anyways. She said in her head.

Chapter 14

Adriana woke up the following morning, hungover and disappointed in herself. Although in the moment, having gone out drinking made her feel better. Yet, she was extremely upset with herself for putting her baby at risk like that. This wasn't the life she wanted for herself. I can't live this way anymore. I just can't, she said in her mind. It was unknown if she had harmed the baby after last night's escapades.

After thinking over the crazy events that went down last night, she picked up the phone to call her gynecologist and made an appointment for the following morning. Then, she texted Stacy the information to meet her over there and mentioned a few facts from last night's awful incidents.

"Adriana! We need to talk before the appointment. I'm going to come over with breakfast in the morning before we head to the doctor, so we can talk," Stacy texted back to her.

"I know. I feel like such a horrible person. Okay, thank you. I'll see you tomorrow," Adriana replied, with a sad emoji.

The rest of the day was spent moping around and spending a lot of time in the bathroom. Her body was very angry with her and she was paying for it. Nothing was doing the trick to cure that hangover. Seven o'clock rolled around and it was almost impossible to keep her eyes open. She gave in and crawled into her pink satin sheets, then pulled the large downy comforter over her head before instantly passing out.

Bright and early, her body woke her up with more runs to the bathroom. It wasn't even five in the morning yet; however, since she fell asleep so early she was ready to start the day. The doctor appointment wasn't until nine. She texted Stacy to come over any time since she was already awake, but she wanted to head out the door by 8:15 for the appointment. Stacy arrived shortly after Adriana texted her; and walked in with bagels, cream cheese and hazelnut coffee from one of their favorite cafés on the island.

"Girl, you have SO much catching me up to do!" Stacy exclaimed. They spent the following 45 minutes catching up over Adriana's crazy trip to New York first. "So yeah, I don't know if her baby is at harm or not now. I can't believe I did that Stacy. I am so upset with myself and disgusted." Stacy rubbed her arm, indicating without words that it was okay for her to do such a crazy thing. "I mean, yes, that was crazy. That was something out of a movie! Let's hope for the best outcome there." Adriana smiled; then they left the house to head to the doctor's office.

The girls were waiting for a few minutes in the lobby after Adriana signed in before she was called into the back. Once she was in the room and the nurse performed several tests, in addition to asking her many personal questions, the doctor walked in.

"Ms. Santos, it's nice to meet you." The Doctor stated as she reached to shake Adriana's hand. "After reviewing your lab work, it does appear you are in fact pregnant. I'd like to have the nurse perform a sonogram on you to check on the baby's status. Do you know how far along you are?"

"I have absolutely no idea, sadly. It was only just a few days ago I discovered I was pregnant. This most certainly was not planned. Also, I know I put my baby at risk the other night." She then went into explaining more details before the nurse rolled in the equipment to examine her.

While the transducer was pressing and moving around on her stomach for several minutes, the sound of a tiny heartbeat overcame the room. Adriana smiled with tears of joy.

"That's your baby, Ms. Santos. And it looks like you're close to 16 weeks and everything looks to be going smoothly. Would you like to know the sex of your baby?"

"16 weeks?! Wow! How did I not know I was pregnant this entire time??" Adriana inquired with disbelief on her face. The nurse went into explaining a few different things before Adriana put up her hand to stop her from talking. Rude. The nurse thought.

"Let's just get back to the part on telling me the sex of my baby." Stacy was holding Adriana's hand and squeezed it as the nurse announced, "It's a girl." As she's printing out photos of the sonogram, the two girls were laughing and giggling over all the excitement.

"She can be a baby model, after you!" Stacy exclaimed.

"I guess I wasn't gaining weight after all, like I originally thought was happening to my body for the last month. Well, that's reassuring," she mentioned to her friend and the nurse. They smiled back to her comment. Adriana got cleaned up and changed back into her clothes before they were out the door, paperwork and photographs in hand. As she pulled into the driveway of her bungalow, she told Stacy, "Thank you so much for coming with me and being a part of this. I was so scared I lost the baby and can't get over the fact I'm having a healthy baby girl growing inside of me now. I'm a bit surprised at how far along I am, and that I had no idea."

"I wouldn't have missed it for the world. I know this isn't the ideal situation for you, but I'm so proud and happy for you. I think this is the change you need in your life."

"I couldn't agree more," Adriana replied. "I think I'm going to go lie down for a bit and take this all in. I'll call you later." She kissed Stacy on the cheek and headed inside the house.

In the kitchen, she rummaged through her junk drawers to find a pink highlighter and pulled it out. Then she searched through one of the sonogram photos and drew a few pink hearts on the front with the highlighter. On the back she wrote "It's a girl", "Due March" and "She's yours" with a signed "A" at the bottom. She found a blank envelope and stuck the sonogram into it, then addressed it to Jim, without writing anything else. Next, she found a stamp to stick on the envelope and walked to the mailbox to stick it in before raising the red flag. She washed her hands of it, before saying "That'll do it." Then went back inside and straight to the couch for a nap.

Several days later, Jim was going through his pile of mail Melanie had placed in their office before he suddenly saw a blank envelope with his name addressed on the front in stylish handwriting. He opened the mail and saw the sonogram. His heart almost jumped out of his chest when he realized it was from Adriana.

"Jim, we need to leave in five minutes for our appointment," Melanie yelled from across the hall. Jim quickly shoved the photo in the middle of one of his books he had stored in the desk drawer and chucked it back in.

They rushed into their car and traveled to the couples counseling appointment.

"Is everything okay? You're acting kind of weird and your face looks rather white," Melanie asked Jim.

"Yeah, no, I'm fine. I guess I'm feeling a little under the weather," he lied. Once they arrived at the therapist's office, they went inside for their hour-long appointment. After it ended, they left the office and got back into the car.

"That was a good session, don't you think?" Melanie asked.

"Yes, dear."

"We have a way to go, but I know it's best for us and our baby on the way." Jim coughed and choked on his own saliva.

"Are you okay?" Melanie questioned, confused by his reaction.

"Yeah, just had a tickle in my throat," Jim lied again. Meanwhile, his mind had a million thoughts of Adriana's pregnancy. He didn't even know how to comprehend all this news at once. It was big information and a lot to accept. What the hell am I going to do?? He replayed over and over in his head. Ignorance and denial were his two favorite words when it came to handling problems. And that was how he chose to handle this enormous news. It wasn't real to him.

Meanwhile, back in Key West, Adriana was wondering if Jim received the sonogram or not. Will I hear from him again? She wasn't holding her breath. It was still hard to believe that any of this was real life. The only people that knew at this point was her friend Kristen and Jim, if he bothered to even check the mail. "I wonder if Melanie knows now? I wonder what happened to her baby..." Adriana questioned out loud.

An email alert sounded off on her phone and as she checked it, she saw it's for a modeling gig in Italy over the course of two weeks. Since her belly was smaller than most women at this stage, she decided to take it. The modeling agency sent over her itinerary showing that her flight was leaving in two days for Milan. There were a few more gigs around Europe she will also participate in while she's out there. This wasn't going to be an easy trip, being pregnant and growing, but she was hoping no one would notice, before she was in too deep. Besides, she still wasn't 100% positive on what she was going to do about the baby. Keep it? Adoption?

Adriana got her bags packed in time before the driver picked her up at ten o'clock on the dot, a couple mornings later. She made it on time to the plane and was in first class, as per usual when she flew for modeling gigs. The flight was rather long and wasn't as easy for her to handle this time around with the pregnancy. Numerous times, she went back and forth to the bathroom to be sick. No champagne this time; and her body was very particular as to which foods she could keep down, or even eat.

The following morning, as the sun was rising, she finally landed in Milan after a quick stop in Paris. It wasn't long before she was off the flight and in the driver's car headed to the hotel.

"Ms. Santos, good morning to you. I have your itinerary for the following weeks to come. I understand you were on a long flight, but it appears I will need to be back at your hotel in merely a couple hours to take you to a photo shoot." Adriana shook her head in disbelief. Although, she wasn't surprised to have to be ready to go that quickly after flying for over 15 hours and hardly resting. This was how the modeling industry went.

"Thank you. Could you please stop at a coffee shop on the way to the hotel?"

"Yes ma'am," the driver responded. She knew it was best for her to skip a nap when she got to the hotel, and instead freshened herself up with caffeine and a shower. Otherwise, she would be one groggy, pregnant mess. Shortly after she picked up a large coffee and checked into her hotel, the driver was already waiting outside to pick her back up. The easy part for her, was that she didn't have to worry about what to wear, do her hair or make-up since they would be handling that at the photo shoot.

On the contrary, this was going to be a long day of photo shoots around historical areas of the city. It would be a lot more exciting if she was well-rested and feeling better. Following this shoot, she would be jetting the following evening to Switzerland. There would only be a couple days in each country to complete the photoshoots before she flew to the next one. According to her itinerary, she would be ending the trip in Paris for a fashion show.

Even though she was traveling to some of the most beautiful places in the world, she felt lonely on the road as a single woman. The limo drivers had been the only people she engaged with, aside from the photographers, make-up artists and the fashion designers. Yet, it was strictly business related and they were different people in each country she traveled to.

Adriana was rather excited to be traveling to Santorini, Greece in the coming days. She already decided to pull an all-nighter while she was there, so she could live it up before she was off to the next country. On a normal modeling trip for her, it was easy meeting other people and spending time in between shoots carousing. However, in her current state and constantly being sick, she wanted nothing more than her hotel bed at the end of every day. Santorini was her only exception.

Photoshoot after photoshoot; make-up contours and glamor; and one dazzling ensemble after the next, she finally made it to Greece and explored every nook and cranny she could within the thirty-six hours she was there. Although twenty of those hours were spent doing photo shoots. The twinkling blue water overlooking the cliffs from the white and indigo buildings, was the most breathtaking location she had ever seen with her own eyes. It was so captivating and picturesque, that it didn't look real. It almost felt as if she were in a real-live desktop wallpaper.

In the blink of an eye, she was already at the Paris fashion show. The chaos behind the curtains caused her so much anxiety that her baby was kicking for the first time. The sequined dresses and outfits were not fitting her the same way now, as her belly had grown ever so slightly. The fashion designers had to tear a few pieces of fabric to fit her, but it was not noticeable to the eye from a distance while she was on the runway. For a thirty-minute fashion show, it felt like an eternity to the models. Before she knew it, the show was finished, and she was already on a plane back to the States.

Chapter 15

Days passed by, which turned into many dissipating months as Jim and Melanie continued with couples counseling and doctor appointments. In addition, Jim was still ignoring the fact that he had another child on the way down in South Florida, and his wife didn't have a clue. As each week passed, it became easier to tell himself that it was probably a cruel joke Adriana did to get his attention. Although, he had endless nightmares of the news several times a week and chose not to confirm if it was true.

Melanie's once small baby bump was now a basketball size belly. They decided not to find out the sex of the baby until he or she was born. She was now only four weeks out from the baby's birth. Melanie had been spending many days and nights getting the nursery ready for their baby's arrival. She decorated it with white's and grey's, and unisex items. Jim hadn't been much help since he was still traveling a lot for work. He was planning on slowing things down closer to the birth day and for several weeks after to help with the baby.

Therapy had helped them considerably move past Jim's infidelity and the traumatic day Melanie encountered when Adriana showed up at their house. It took Melanie many months to feel safe again in their house while Jim was out of town. They paid extra money for a far better security system. The new one they had installed has cameras around the house, the interior and exterior, as well as a video camera in the doorbell. It could be monitored by an app on their cell phone and one could even lock down the house with one button on there. It was very high tech and helped Melanie feel safe at home alone.

It was the early morning of a Fall day in November, the sixth to be exact, when Melanie felt severe contractions at two in the morning. It was three weeks too early for her to be having the baby. Hurriedly, she got out of bed, threw on some clothes and drove herself to the emergency room at the local hospital. Jim was in D.C. on a business trip so she called his cell phone.

"Hey babe, everything okay?" He answered with a groggy voice.

"I'm having really bad contractions and am going to the hospital. I don't know if something is wrong or..." Suddenly the seat was soaking wet, "I'm having the baby. Which seems to be the case now because I'm pretty sure my water just broke."

"Ah, babe! Seriously? Holy cow I wasn't expecting this already. Alright, let me check on flights back home. Let me know what's going on when you get to the hospital. I love you babe! I'm so excited, but I want to be there with you and will do my damnedest to find a way there as fast as I can."

Melanie smiled and replied, "I'll call you once I'm there and know what is happening."

When she hung up the phone, Jim jumped on his laptop to check direct flights for later that morning. He found a flight for a reasonable price leaving at six, which would get him in around nine. As he was looking, Melanie texted him "Looks like we are having a baby today!". I really hope this baby doesn't arrive before I get there. He thought while booking the flight. Jim spent the next couple hours packing up his things and sending emails to cancel meetings, as well as informing his team what was going on. Melanie texted him close to four in morning, "Baby is looking good, and they want me to start pushing in a couple hours. Hope you'll make it for baby's arrival. Xoxo."

Jim replied, "I'm headed straight there from the airport. Tell baby to slow it down for me. I love you!"

Melanie and Jim's parents showed up to the hospital with flowers and balloons. "Oh honey! You're going to be a Mom soon!" Her mom exclaimed with excitement. At this point, Melanie was in a complete fog from the pain. Jim's parents decided to say their Hello's, then wait in the lobby area. They were an odd couple and quite judgmental, which made it very hard for Melanie to ever build a relationship with them. She was glad that they chose to wait outside.

The nurse walked into the room to check on Melanie. "It looks like we are moving right along for the epidural. Are you ready to get started?" she asked Melanie.

"Yes, please. I'm in so much pain."

The nurse injected the numbing medication, and took the needle and catheter to perform the rest of the epidural. "I'll come back in a little bit to check on you again and then it'll be go time."

As the nurse left the room, Melanie looked at the clock to see that it was now a little after eight. "Honey, what time will Jim be here?" Her mother asked.

"I believe he lands close to nine. We are about thirty minutes from the airport, so I hope he's here before 9:30 and this baby isn't here yet."

"Do you want me to stay in the room while you push in case he isn't here yet?"

"Yes, I suppose so. I don't want to do this alone."

The medicine had still not kicked in and Melanie was curled in the fetal position as each contraction occurred. "Ohhhh, I need this epidural to take my pain away already!" Right as she was shrieking in pain, Kristen rushed into the room. "Oh, thank goodness you haven't had the baby yet! I was so afraid I already missed it," she shrieked while running up to Melanie before hugging her.

"I'm so happy for you! How much longer until you start pushing?"

"I'm not really sure, maybe an hour."

They chit-chat back and forth for several minutes when Melanie's father walked in with a cheeseburger and fries. The whiff of the food almost caused Melanie to vomit immediately. "Dad! Please get that out of here. That smell is not at all enticing to me this early in the morning."

While he's taking a huge bite of the burger, he quickly turned back around and went out the door. Jim's mother pulled out a small travel size Lysol can and sprayed it around the room in disgust.

Jim ran into her Dad and knocked the fries all over the floor. "Sorry about that Mr. Johnson!" He said while collecting the fries off the floor.

"Ah, no worries son. Now go in and see your wife." Jim sprinted through the door and immediately kissed Melanie on the forehead before she even realized who it was.

"We're having a baby!" Jim eagerly blurted.

"Yes, we are!" She excitedly answered. "And you're early," she smiled. It wasn't too soon after Jim's arrival that the nurse returned to the room. She checked to see how far along Melanie was before stating, "Alright Mrs. Benton, it's time to start pushing." Both Jim and Melanie's parents came over to hug them, say their I love you's, then headed out to the waiting area. The birthing process was unfortunately not a quick one for them. Melanie was in labor for a solid ten hours before a baby girl popped out. "It's a girl!" The Doctor called out. Jim kissed Melanie on the forehead and tears welled up in his eyes. It was very rare for Jim to get emotional.

In the lobby, a baby chime emitted out of the speakers, indicating that a baby had been born. Seconds after, Jim ran out shouting, "It's a girl!" He grabbed his head in astonishment, and everyone clapped. His parents then rushed up to him and gave him an endearing hug. There wasn't a dry eye in the room.

"And her name?" His mother-in-law asked.

"Annabelle Elizabeth Benton," he replied before rushing back into the room.

Melanie spent the next couple of days recovering, being shown how to handle a newborn and how to breastfeed. Both inexperienced parents were exhausted, and they were finally on their way home with the newest addition to the family. Melanie and Jim's parents were already there waiting. Their moms decorated the front door with pink colors and signs of the baby's arrival. As Jim, Melanie and the baby showed up and walked in the door with Annabelle, Buddy and Bella immediately ran up to smell this new "thing" entering the house. Both their tails were wagging in excitement and confusion. It didn't take long before they became acquainted with her and were licking her toes.

Over the following weeks of long days with no sleep, and much needed coffee, their little girl was growing so fast. Melanie kept up with her growth by taking photos next to cutesy signs showing "One Month", "Two Months", and so forth. She created an album on the internet where she could share the pictures with family and friends. It was still hard to believe that she and Jim were parents now. Their entire life had changed.

After the months passed and they were in a good routine, Melanie was finally ready to bring Annabelle out in the public on her own. Annabelle could now accompany her on trips to the grocery store and other shops. It most certainly wasn't an easy task, but she eventually got the hang of it. Every day became easier and easier for her while Jim was away. He was still travelling more frequently than she anticipated. At times, it seemed as if she were a single mom due to Jim's lack of presence. At least it felt that way.

Jim, on the contrary, was such an amazing Dad to Annabelle. Much more than Melanie predicted. Every time he came home, which was now every weekend, he took over all the responsibilities so Melanie could do as she pleased. They were also lucky enough to have the help from both their families to babysit anytime they needed. It was hard getting out of the house, but once a month they made sure to go on dates together to have a little bit of alone time, and peace and quiet.

Melanie felt more alive than ever in the following months after the birth of Annabelle and she had become more active. Her body quickly bounced back and she was in better shape now than before. This was from all the runs she went on with Annabelle in her stroller each morning. Also, during her nap times, Melanie has been able to sneak in a work out using the videos on the internet. This helped keep her mind straight and beat the postpartum depression. Life was really looking up for her, and for her marriage, too. She couldn't recall the last time she felt this happy in her life. For the first time in a long time, she could hear the birds singing more often and the sun was shining brighter. Even the flowers looked radiant in brighter shades of pink and purple, and were blooming more than she had ever recognized previously during Spring. Everything around her felt more flourishing and beautiful. Life was good.

Chapter 16

The pregnancy was not getting any easier for Adriana to go through alone. Not having any one there to help her or take care of her was draining. The morning sickness phase had at least passed but carrying around heavy weight all the time was a lot to handle. She had to put her modeling career on hold because she wasn't offered any pregnancy gigs. Luckily, she had enough money in her savings to not work for several months.

Adriana had been contemplating what to do about the baby; and now more than ever since she was six months along. The thought of raising a child as a single mother terrified her. Yet, she was way passed the point of an abortion. As time went on, with her belly growing, she began thinking adoption may be her best choice in this situation. The process was going to be hard to go through one way or another. She got on her computer to Google adoption.

While looking through all the different sites, the stress and emotions overcame her. How can I go through this? She thought to herself. It was in that moment she realized it was probably be best to see a therapist to help her work through all the feelings and to decide what was best. If she gave up her baby up for adoption, then this would take a huge toll on her. After researching several adoption agencies and therapists, she picked up the phone to call a few.

"Hello? Yes, hi. I am wondering if you all are accepting new patients?"

"Yes, ma'am, we are."

"Ok, wonderful. Is it possible I could get an appointment tomorrow afternoon?"

"Actually, we have an opening Thursday at 9 AM."

"Perfect. I'll take that. Thank you." She ended the call after providing the lady with all her details, then stared blankly at her phone. This was really happening. She had to make a choice to do what was right for her baby, and soon. Adriana knew she wasn't in the right head space to raise a child alone. This wasn't how she pictured her life going. At only twenty-seven years old, she thought by now she would be married and having children with a husband.

She pondered; How did my life turn into this? Why did I meet Jim and continue this affair? I don't understand why it had to go this way for me. Maybe it's true what they all say about karma. Maybe I deserve this for being the "other woman". Now he gets the happy life with his wife, and their baby, and I'm a miserable single woman that's pregnant with his child. I want my life to turn around, but I am miserable. I really hope therapy will help.

The days had been drifting by her so fast, and not hearing from Jim any longer was still so heartbreaking. She had made more attempts to get in contact with him, but he had either blocked her or changed his phone number since she received the papers. Ever since the restraining order had been served on her, it had been intimidating for her to reach out to him. She really wanted to know if he received the letter with the sonogram. A part of her was hoping after some time, that he would have dropped the order. Or even maybe missed her enough to get back in touch. Sadly, neither seemed to be true for her.

When she arrived at the therapist's office, her stomach became queasy. She walked in, and waited in the lobby area. There were two brown sofas and a few chairs around the walls. It was a bit dingy and not at all what she expected for this type of environment. The Doctor called her back and started by asking her numerous questions. She instantly became flooded by old memories as she begun talking, then started crying before blurting out her entire life story to this stranger.

Adriana went into a brief narrative of her childhood, then her affair with Jim and the idea of adoption. It was during the middle of her session, that it hit her. After saying everything out loud and discussing the baby girl growing inside of her, she realized there was no way she could give her up. And just like that, she changed her tone and talked about the possible future of raising a child alone, as a single mother and as a model. The session went over by fifteen minutes before the therapist found a good time to pause the session.

"I would like to schedule you on weekly appointments."

"I think that's a good idea as well," Adriana responded.

As she walked out of the Doctor's office, she headed towards the receptionist's desk and booked as many openings as she could over the course of a few months. On her drive back home, she rolled the window down and felt the wind blow through her long locks. All she listened to was the gusts of air. It was a peaceful moment feeling the breeze against her golden skin. Once she arrived home, she went straight out to the patio. It was a beautiful day for the windows to be open; there was a crisp bit of coolness in the air. The French doors remained open while she was lying in her hammock, overlooking the water.

While rubbing her belly, she begun talking to her little girl growing inside, telling her she was going to change her entire life in a positive way. Her eyes slowly shut until she woke up to her cell phone buzzing in her pocket. She looked down and saw it was her friend Nicole.

"Hey girl, you still free for lunch?" Adriana had completely forgotten her lunch plans with her friend.

"Yes, actually. I'm glad you reached out. Let's go to that cute place by the water. Sea Legs Café I believe it's called?".

Nicole replied, "Sounds great, meet you at 1 PM?".

"Yes ma'am, see you there."

Luckily, there was still another hour before she had to leave to meet her friend at the restaurant. Slowly, she got out of the hammock and went out to the dock. As she stood at the end, she closed her eyes and inhaled a big deep breath, then exhaled in full force. While her eyes remained closed, she spoke to the universe through the wind, asking for help in raising her child alone and asking for reassurance that she was making the right decision. As she opened her eyes through her next exhalation, a beautiful dark red, orange and blue spotted butterfly zoomed around her.

The butterfly flew right near her above the water, then circled back and fluttered around in front before landing on her ring finger. She smiled while looking down at him, too eager to move a muscle. Seconds later, he fluttered off down the coast. Without warning, her baby carried out a sensational kick. Adriana was grinning from ear to ear, when happy tears fell from her eyes as she said, "Thank you."

She walked back into the house, leaving the doors open. When she got in, she jumped on her laptop to look up nursery furniture and started a list of all the items she needed to purchase. The next thing she wanted to do was go through the items in the second bedroom and clear it out for the nursery. There were only a mere few months before her little one was arriving. A trip to Baby's R Us and Target were on the near horizon; possibly even after lunch with her friend if she felt up for it.

Once she wrote down some things on her agenda, she examined her closest for clothes. She didn't realize her belly was outgrowing all her outfits faster than she could keep up. Another item to add to the list. Pregnancy clothes. She thought to herself. It was almost as if the last several months weren't even real and it just hit her that she was pregnant. Since there was enough time before meeting Nicole, she decided to take a quick shower then head out.

Adriana arrived before her friend, and had the host seat her at the table. She ordered a sparkling water, while patiently waiting for her friend, who was now ten minutes late. Nicole rushed in and to the table Adriana was sitting at. "I'm so sorry I'm late! I had to take care of a business call."

"Oh, don't worry about it. I am in no rush," she replied and laughed, while pointing to her belly. Nicole giggled back and hugged her. "I haven't seen you since that photoshoot we did over in Barbados. That was like a year ago now, right?" Nicole questioned. "Wow! Has it seriously been that long?? Goodness. So much has changed in my life since then!" Adriana then caught her up on everything while they ate their lunch over the course of a few hours before saying their goodbyes.

Adriana choose to make a run to a high-end maternity store with more fashionable clothes for her growing belly. She spent a few hundred dollars on clothes that stretched to different sizes but could also be worn even after the pregnancy. After shopping, she made another pit stop at a baby store to open a registry for those that were planning on sending her gifts, since she decided against having an official baby shower.

When she entered the store, she went straight to the customer service counter to speak to someone about a registry. After the lady asked and received all the information she needed from her, she handed over a portable scanner to Adriana, so she could walk around and easily select all the items she wanted added to her list. Adriana explored the store and clicked on random items at one point because it felt like a fun shopping spree. Beep after beep sounds alerted, as she kept scanning items. As she looked around, she saw several others were doing the same thing as her, but as a couple. It brought a measure of sadness to her as she thought about doing this alone.

The thoughts were really hitting home for her. Although she knew she was raising her child alone, she didn't realize how much it bothered her until now. Her excitement from initially walking into the store had now turned into sorrow. She no longer had the motivation to pick out any other items, so, she decided to leave. While driving back home, she thought about Jim, wishing he was a part of all this with her. Her mind reminisced to memories they shared together.

Chapter 17

A year ago, Jim and Adriana were at this beautiful luxury resort in Napa Valley. Adriana was flying back to the States from a modeling gig in Japan and had a layover in San Francisco. She was scheduled to originally fly from there back to the East Coast, but instead she stayed around to meet with Jim. Jim had scheduled his itinerary around meeting her at the airport, so they could drive into the valley. Her flight landed around 9:15 that Friday morning. He was staying in the city earlier that week and drove to the airport to pick her up. He rented a red classic and sleek old '56 Chevy convertible. It was bright and shiny, with a white convertible top. The interior had leather seats with a red and white finish.

The sun glistened off the rims and the chrome lines along each side, as well as the door handles. He pulled up with the top down, and the Beach Boys blasting through the speakers. It was like something you'd see in a movie. Adriana thought, how was that my life? That was truly incredible. "Well hello there gorgeous!" Jim yelled out. She intentionally wore a black dress with white polka dots on her flight, for that magical moment. Jim told her the day before that he was going to rent one of those classy cars. It only seemed appropriate to play into the fairytale they were going to be in over the weekend. She even purchased a pair of vintage round Paris Chanel sunglasses to go along with the theme.

The long curls in her hair bounced up and down in coils as she skipped towards the car. Jim popped the trunk then jumped over the driver's door without opening it. She stood there with her sparkling red high heels together, holding her black Chanel purse in the middle of her body with both hands. She released her grip on the right side of her purse and reached up to her sunglasses; then pulled her specs down ever so slightly, where Jim could see her eyes, and gave him a quick wink. He could see her alluring green eyes sparkle with her provocative cat eye makeup. Her index finger pushed her specs back up her nose and her shimmering red lips blew him a kiss.

Jim picked up her Louis Vuitton luggage and carefully placed it in the trunk, then shut it tightly. He ran around the passenger's side of the car and opened the door. "Madam," he stated while motioning her with his hands to step into the car. Adriana slowly strutted herself towards him and into the car. A sweet, sensual aroma rose off her body and swiftly blew by him. He let out a loud, sexual sigh. Delicately, he closed the door behind her and ran around back to the driver's side, jumping over the door again.

The white, fluffy clouds in the blue skies reflected off his Ray Bans. Wispy, long curls waved in the wind by each mile marker. The sound of the air was blowing in their ears as they traveled down the highway. They were both smiling from ear to ear. Jim reached over for Adriana's hand, and held it ever so tightly. He squeezed her hand three times, indicating he loved her with non-verbal language. She squeezed back four times. The drive took close to two hours as they hit traffic along the way. A couple miles before their destination, they saw the displayed signs, pointing them in the direction towards the luxury ranch resort.

The butterflies of excitement rapidly flew around in Adriana's stomach, as they approached closer and closer to their final stop. Numerous bright and colorful trees were surrounding the resort, some tall, reaching into the sky, while others were shorter and groomed to perfection. The clouds were rolling in low, yet still above the taller trees. She looked up into the sky, and caught a whiff of the crisp mountain air in the valley. They continued driving over a small bridge, towards the entrance, which was surrounded by more trees.

Jim drove slowly through the forest, as they each took in the appealing landscape. The ranch was nestled in the middle of the forest, with open space between the valleys. Smaller shrubs and plants were placed perfectly around the entrance and along the exterior of the floor to ceiling windows. The facade of the ranch was a variety of greys and beige stones surrounding the building. He pulled the Chevy up towards the entryway.

"I'll go get us checked in babe, stay right here." He walked up the three steps and opened the glass door. People were cozied up near the fireplace in the right side of the lobby. Towards the left side were two free standing desks also made of stone. Two ladies were standing behind each desk on a computer, in all black suits. A gentleman immediately approached Jim with a tray in his hand holding a variety of red and white wines.

"Can I interest you in a glass, sir?" Jim reached his hand out to take a glass of the red wine.

"Thank you." As he approached the desk, both women smiled at Jim and looked him directly in the eye.

"Good afternoon, sir. Are you checking in today?" The blonde agent responded.

"Yes, hello. Jim Benton." While she looked him up in their system, he pulled out his ID and credit card. "Oh yes, Mr. Benton. I see you are staying for two nights, is that correct?" Jim gave a head nod while sipping on his wine.

"I have you staying in our Estate Lodge, which is located here," she stated while pointing on the map of the premises. After swiping his card, and completing the process on her computer, she handed over the room keys. "Enjoy your stay with us Mr. Benton," she said while giving him a wink. He put the keys in his pocket and walked back towards the front door. On his way out, he snagged a glass of white wine. Then used his arms and back to push open the door.

"My dear. Here you are," he greeted, while handing over the wine to Adriana.

"Why thank you, sexy." Jim opened the driver door this time to get back into the car; then followed the instructions over to their private estate lodge. In the distance from the lodge, they could see the entire estate was made from wooden planks. The wooden stairs led up to the entrance of the lodge. He pulled the car off to the side in a gravel area.

When he turned the car off, Adriana jumped out of her seat in excitement.

She rushed out of the car, and stood there looking up at the lodge, while smiling. She then closed her eyes, and did a twirl, taking in the fresh breathable air. "Ahhhh. This is the life." Jim ran up behind her and scooped her up in his arms. He carried her up the stairs and walked over through the rather large and spacious patio. Carefully, he laid her down on the white cushioned love seat, then kissed her passionately, taking her breath away.

Heat rose from their bodies in excitement. Jim lifted her dress and forced her legs open. As he caught a glimpse of her red, lacey underwear, a bulge grew in his pants. She placed her hand onto his package, causing him to groan. His mouth was salivating at the thought of tasting her again. He quickly pulled down her underwear, and began tasting her. The moans coming out of her mouth echoed throughout the rocks along the hill. As he was pleasuring her, he reached to unzip his pants. Rapidly pulling his pants halfway down and taking her right there. She felt every inch of him inside her. After several minutes passed, they simultaneously moaned at the peak of their mutual orgasm.

Sweat was pouring down the back of Jim's shirt as he collapsed on her from the gratifying exhaustion.

"I love you," she whispered in his ear. He kissed her on the cheek in response. Seconds passed by before he got up, adjusted himself and pulled his pants back up. "I'll get the bags out of the car," he stated while walking away. Adriana felt a combination of contentment from the orgasm, mixed with a feeling of disappointment. She didn't like how he used her body like that, then walked off showing no emotions. Something didn't feel right about it, but she didn't want to dwell on it in that moment.

She pulled her underwear back up and fixed her dress. While sitting on the outdoor love seat, she glanced around at her surroundings. The deck fence was wired through planks of wood. Under the pergola, draped with white curtains, was a stone-walled fireplace. A bottle of Merlot was precisely placed on the outdoor wooden tray that sat on the granite coffee table. Over to the left was a bouquet of sunflowers was beautifully presented in a crystal vase on the end table.

Adriana stood up and walked around the patio, taking in and observing each piece of elegance surrounding her. She then walked around the side of the lanai towards the front door. Jim already had the door open and was placing their luggage in the master bedroom. As she walked through the front door, she caught a whiff of fresh cedar. The lodge was breathtaking. Her senses were over-stimulated.

The grand entrance led to the living room, which was an open floor plan towards the kitchen, as well. It was hard to miss the enormous stone fireplace that was the focal point of the living room. The stones continued up the wall towards the top of the vaulted ceiling. There was a cozy, comfortable feel to the room with the whites, greys and beige colors of the furniture. The white kitchen cabinets had stone knobs distinctly placed in them. Dark grey and white sparkles shined through the granite countertop. There was a stainless-steel sink in the middle of the island that fit in seamlessly. As Adriana walked through, she slid her hand along the counter to feel the smoothness in the material.

She continued passing through, towards the master bathroom that she came across first. A massive, marble bathtub sat in the center of the room. It was facing the floor to ceiling windows that overlooked a private lanai which was fenced by plants. Glass doors led to the stand-up shower with the rainfall shower-head. More grey marble slabs were surrounding the floor and the walls. The marble gleamed in beauty. Even the lavatory was enclosed with marble. Adriana walked through the other door that led to the master bedroom.

The private balcony was immediately noticeable through the grand windows as you entered the room. There was a private Jacuzzi on their balcony that overlooked the nature preserves. She breezed right past Jim to open the French doors to their patio.

"Ahhhh, just take it all in babe. I can't get over this magical place," she said while closing her eyes and smiling.

"Hun, let's go get a bite to eat," Jim suggested. Adriana rolled her eyes without him seeing.

"Okay, we can do that." She was becoming more upset by his actions but didn't want to let that affect her mood in the moment.

She pulled out her makeup bag from her luggage and walked back to the master bathroom to freshen up. Down the hallway, Jim yelled, "I'll meet you outside, babe." Shaking her head, she remained silent. Tears were welling up in her eyes while she reapplied mascara and red lipstick.

As she was closing the door behind her from the main entrance, she saw Jim texting on his phone. I wonder if he's texting his wife, she thought to herself. This time, Jim didn't get out to open the door for her. What just happened? Why does he go from one extreme mood or moment, to a completely different one? She continued thinking to herself. At this point, she was over analyzing every little thing. Then began feeling more insecure about herself.

He threw on his Ray Bans and started the engine. Jim knew his way around the valley, almost a little too much, which made Adriana wonder how many other women he had brought here too. They drove through the valley, not speaking to each other and only listening to more of the Beach Boys. A café, that looked like a small cabin, was up the road from their lodge. While parking, Jim looked at his phone stating,

"Damn, not sure I can get service here, either."

Adriana looked back at him, "Is there some kind of important business call you need to make or something?"

Irritated, he replied, "Yeah, something like that." It was rather obvious he was lying.

Once he parked the car, she instantly got out and slammed the door. Each heel clicked faster and faster as she approached the café. Jim got out of the car, still looking at his phone for service.

"I'll be in in a second, babe." She didn't even look back or acknowledge his comment. Subsequently, he glanced back down at this phone and noticed he had one bar of service. From his speed dial list, he clicked on Melanie's name and the phone rang.

"Hi babe. Did you make it to Sacramento?" Melanie answered.

"Yes, Hun. My service is awful out here though, so I may not be in touch as much. I just need to tie up some loose ends with these clients to make sure they're not jumping ship, then I'll be back out Sunday night."

"Sure, I understand that. You are such a dedicated business man. One of the many reasons I love you. I'm glad you made it there safely. Keep in touch when you can. I love you."

He clicked to end the call without saying he loved her back. While walking up towards the café, he went inside and saw Adriana standing with her arms crossed. It was apparent she was upset with him. He wrapped his arm around her waist and kissed her on the cheek.

"Sorry babe, had to take care of a business call." Her intuition was saying otherwise, but she let it go.

The host seated them to a private table in the back of the café. The two of them looked overly dressed for a place such as that. After being seated, a waitress approached them with menus.

"Good afternoon. Can I get you two anything to drink?" Jim immediately responded, "Yes, I'll get a glass of your Chianti wine." Adriana was looking over at him while he ordered, thinking how un-gentleman like that was of him.

"And for you ma'am?" She let out an audible sigh,

"I'll have what he's having." The waitress scribbled down on her notepad and stepped away.

Jim worked up an appetite from their quick session earlier. Yet, Adriana did not have much of an appetite, given this uncomfortable gut feeling she had. Neither one of them said anything to each other, and stared at the menu. The waitress delivered their glasses of wine, inquiring,

"Do either of you know what you would like, or would you like me to go over our specials?"

It only took a matter of seconds, before Jim replied, "I'll get the steak sandwich and a side of your French onion soup." While jotting down his request, Adriana got up from the table.

"Oh, just get me a Caesar salad, thanks," she furiously stated while marching off. She stormed into the women's restroom and straight into a stall.

Chapter 18

Over the following months, Adriana finished decking out the nursery. It looked as if pink threw up all over the place. Her mother flew in from Italy to be with her during the month her baby was due. She also planned to spend the following months helping her out after she was born.

"Have you thought of the little one's name, dear?" Her mother asked.

"Yes, I've been toying with Isabella Anna or Milania Anna, but I'm still deciding. I'm waiting on a sign to tell me which one to go with."

"Well, those are both beautiful. And I love that you are using my middle name as her middle name," her mother replied smiling.

Since Adriana decided not to have a baby shower, she still sent out the announcement to all her close friends and family, as well as the information where she was registered. She didn't really like the whole cliché of having a shower and playing the cheesy games, then opening all the gifts in front of everyone. Plus, she was going through this alone and it just felt different. Boxes from Amazon, Bed Bath and Beyond,

Target, Baby's R Us and other companies kept showing up at her front door. Her mother helped her keep track of who got her what, so she could send thank you notes.

The nursery was filled with items and was almost complete for her baby's arrival. Her neighborhood dumpster was overflowing with cardboard boxes and the packaging from all the items she has received. The last item she was waiting on was a high-tech baby stroller she ordered on line from one of those fancy retailers. This stroller was white and black with rose gold chassis. The wheels had a 360-degree swivel and breaks on the rear wheels. The baskets had magnetic lids and the leather made it easy to wipe up spills. Even the seat pad came with a five-point safety harness and the handlebar was adjustable to three positions. It was the trendiest, and one of the most expensive, strollers on the market.

A couple weeks later, the stroller finally arrived. Her mother assisted in putting the pieces together for her, since Adriana was quite helpless at that point. Her belly had expanded so far that reaching for anything on the floor was nearly impossible. Over the following days, it began to feel more surreal to her. Any day now, her house would no longer be quiet and with only her living in it. Pretty soon it would be filled with a lot of chaos for a while, yet a lot of memories, too. She was anxious and excited at the same time for her daughter's arrival. While day dreaming, she glanced into the nursery and around the room.

Adriana rubbed her belly as she walked around the room looking at everything. In the crib was a pink little teddy bear that she picked up and saw the tag that read "Bella". She smiled, then said aloud, "Isabella Anna. That's her name."

Her mother overheard her speaking from the other room, then yelled out, "What?"

Adriana walked out of the room gripping onto the teddy bear. "Her name, I've decided, will be Isabella Anna." Just as her mom rushed over to hug her, liquid gushed out from under Adriana's sundress to the floor.

"Oh, my goodness! That scared the living daylight out of me!" She screeched to her mom.

"Let's go. Baby Isabella is on her way!" Her mother took the bag she had already packed for the hospital, and rushed Adriana into the car, swerving around car after car, before finally arriving to the hospital. It was the middle of the afternoon, a couple weeks into March. Nurses and doctors took her in right away, and to everyone's surprise, Isabella was born an hour after Adriana entered the hospital. The delivery was much easier than she anticipated. Somehow, she even managed to go through the entire process without any drugs.

Adriana's mother stood by her side for the entire birth. Afterwards as well, sleeping on the cardboard like chairs that were in the room, not leaving her side. Luckily, it was only a couple days of that before they could take her baby home. She was so thankful for her mother being by her side and helping her through all this. There's no way she could have possibly done this alone.

The following weeks were very stressful on Adriana. Isabella was not taking to her breasts, so she quickly switched her to formula for ease of convenience. Sleep was completely out of the equation since her daughter was crying almost every other hour of each evening. It was hard to even recognize that Adriana was a model in the state she was looking. Her hair was hardly ever combed, she only showered every few days, if that. Several of her friends dropped by to meet Isabella, but Adriana did not allow them to stay for very long since she felt like a hot mess. Her mother had helped as much as possible, but it was coming to that time she would need to get back overseas to work.

"I don't know how I am going to do this without you, Mom," Adriana cried on her mother's shoulder. "This is so hard."

Her mother rubbed her back and held her. "You're going to be just fine. I know you can do this. I am only a phone call away. Even though I know I can't get here fast enough in most cases with the travel time. I'm going to try and come back in a month or two if I can, okay?" Adriana nodded her head.

The taxi arrived at Adriana's house a couple days later to pick up her mother for her flight back to Italy. They hugged on the front stoop, for what seemed like several minutes but was only fifteen seconds.

"I love you sweetie. I'll miss you both. I'll call you once I land." Off her mother went in the cab. Adriana held Isabella tightly in her arms as she watched her mother leave. As she was crying, her daughter began crying and then screaming. She sighed and walked inside to play the game of figuring out why she was crying.

The stress overcame her more and more as each day passed that she was doing it alone. Her house was a complete disaster. Dirty diapers were overflowing in the garbage can. Food was rotting in her fridge. She didn't even recognize herself in the mirror anymore. She became so overwhelmed, that she wasn't sure if she could do it anymore.

"How could I think such a horrible thing?" It was confusing to her how she could love her daughter so much, but also despise her in a way because of how much the baby had drastically changed her life. Adriana did some research on her feelings and discovered she was not alone in the way she felt. There were many other women out also going through the same struggles as her.

It motivated her to join this group of newly single moms to bond with. They met every week, with their babies on hand in strollers, at a coffee shop down the road from Adriana's house. These ladies instantly became close friends of hers. She formed a special bond with most of them since they all seemed to feel similar emotions as herself. It wasn't long before she was back to feeling like herself again. A routine was finally put in place with feeding Isabella and putting her to bed. And she was now cleaning often, as well as taking care of herself.

She admitted that taking care of herself was a much-needed priority, not only for her, but for her daughter. She wanted to be a better person for her daughter. A shower consisted of only a few minutes, but at least they were daily when Isabella was napping. Each day was rather habitual but was becoming easier and easier to manage. Somehow, she also managed to squeeze in some workouts. One of the local gyms on the island, had a day care. This made it much easier for her, so she didn't have to find a babysitter. Her friends were only available every so often to help watch Isabella. There were days she would pat herself on the back for pulling this off alone with no help.

Jim was not far off in the distance of her thoughts and memories. It was hard not to look at her daughter and see him in her almost every single day. The more Isabella grew, the more she recognized his features in her. She often wondered how he was doing, if he was still with Melanie, and if they had a baby or not. That was still an unknown mystery if their baby was even okay, after what she had done. It was hard to believe how long ago it was that she followed through with such an atrocious plan. That person she was, was not even remotely close to who she was today. Does he think of me? Or ever miss me? I wonder if he realizes his daughter was born and was now crawling. Some days, the thoughts haunted her more than others.

Adriana continued going to therapy and was fortunate enough to have her friend Stacy watch Isabella here and there when she went to the appointments. Therapy was helping her tremendously. It was improving her bad behavioral patterns she had developed over the years. In addition, she was becoming a better version of herself, as well as moving past the events from her affair with Jim and what she did to Melanie. She was getting closer and closer to being ready to date; but, sometimes it was hard to even fathom seeing someone again. Jim was the man she envisioned spending her life with. That door had been closed and was so far away, that she barely even saw it anymore. But she refused to stop holding onto the belief, that someday her prince charming would magically appear.

Chapter 19

Summer was already approaching in New York. The air was warm and the cool air had dissipated. It was a nice change of pace from the brutal Winter and cold Spring they had. The trees blooms appeared to turn from browns to greens. Melanie's birthday was coming up later in the week of that balmy, first week of June. Kristen told her not to make plans on that Thursday since she wanted to take her out for her birthday, just the two of them. A night away from Jim and Annabelle. Jim had been around more often than normal since he was able to switch his schedule and was working from home more. It was nice for Melanie having his help with the little one, but it was also a bit crowding. Melanie had become so used to doing things on her own, since much of the time he was out traveling.

He offered to watch Annabelle on the night she had planned with Kristen, so she could go have a fun girls' night for her birthday. On her actual birthday, he had already made reservations at a fancy steakhouse in the city for them. His mother also offered to watch Annabelle that night, so they could celebrate together on a romantic date.

As Thursday rolled around, Melanie began getting all dolled up in a satin black dress that fell to her knees. Not only did she do her hair, but she also put makeup on. College was the last time she got all dressed up like this for a night on the town. At quarter after six, someone knocked on the door. Jim opened it to see a limo driver holding a tray with a glass of champagne.

"Good evening sir. I am looking for Melanie."

Jim looked at the man and laughed that Kristen had set this up for her. "Honey! Your ride is here," he yelled up the stairs.

"I'll be right down," she bellowed back. It wasn't too soon after that she came waltzing down the stairs. Jim watched each step she took, thinking how amazingly beautiful she was. When did he stop noticing how stunning his wife was? No time for thinking about that right now, he thought over to himself. He darted to the end of the stairwell to take her hand, and helped guide her down the last step. Then whispered in her ear, "You look gorgeous, my love. I hope you have a wonderful time with your friend." Melanie grinned at his comment and chill bumps formed all over her neck, shoulders and arms after he kissed her cheek.

Once she departed the house, she took the glass of champagne off the tray the limo driver was holding, then took a sip and smiled. "Thank you. Is Kristen in the limo?" She asked the driver, as they both walked towards the long car.

"We are going to pick her up from here, ma'am." He opened the door and assisted her into the limo, then shut the door behind her. Neon blue hues were shining underneath the all black leather seats. The bar was sparkling with white and clear crystals sitting on top of it, and where the stainless-steel tin held the bottle of champagne chilling on ice. A Happy Birthday sign was hanging along the bottom of the bar with confetti all over the floor. Balloons were also clinging to various areas of the ceiling. As she looked up, she saw a sunroof above her head.

"Oh, this can be fun," she said out loud.

Melanie continued sipping on her bubbly as they approached Kristen's house. In all her excitement, Kristen was already out the door and into the limo before the driver could greet her at the door with champagne. He rolled down the divider window,

"Ladies, are you ready for your adventure?"

Both girls screamed, "Yes!" He turned up the music and the party got started. The first bottle of champagne went down like water for them. Bottle number two was already opened and half empty as they entered the city. The city was so magical. No matter how many times Melanie had been in New York City, it still made her heart race in excitement. It felt like her 21st birthday all over again.

The city lights twinkled in her eyes as she rolled down the window. She closed her eyes and could smell the hot dog stands that were out earlier in the day. When she opened her eyes in awe, they pulled up to a Gatsby inspired restaurant that had a charming bar inside. Kristen always knew how much Melanie loved the Gatsby era. Right before they were to exit the limo, her friend pulled out two feather and sequined headbands for them to wear to complement their dresses. Melanie's heart and stomach could not stop smiling in excitement. The driver opened their door, and helped each of them out of the limo.

"Ladies, I will be here for your next adventure after dinner. Enjoy."

Kristen knocked on the large, wooden door three times. The little window in the door opened and all they could see was a lady's brown eyes through the black mask covering her face.

"Password please," she firmly stated.

Kristen quickly replied, "Gold digger." Just like that, the lady shut the flap and the huge door opened. A puff of smoke clouded the entry way as they entered the dark chamber-esque room. A host approached them, already knowing their names from the reservation that was booked, and escorted them to their table. The restaurant was not like any other that Melanie had ever seen.

It was very dark and grungy inside, but in a fancy and elegant way. The sheer curtains had twinkling lights, and speckles of glitter gleamed around the entire joint. Votive candles were placed on each table, and Victorian wall sconces shined with a plethora of petite torches along every wall. When they received their menus, and glanced over the food choices, it looked very eclectic. Even the drinks were specially hand-made and old-fashioned cocktails.

The ladies took their time ordering food and sipping on their fancy cocktails, truly taking in every bit of charm surrounding them. Shortly after finishing dinner, and a couple blended beverages later, they departed the mysterious speakeasy back into the city of lights. Manuel was already there waiting, standing outside the driver's door of the limo. He bowed his head down in acknowledgement of their presence,

"Ladies. Ready for the next destination?" Melanie looked at Kristen and smirked in eagerness. They both giggled as they practically fell into the limo.

The next stop they landed at was a psychic's shop. Next to the shop was a mucky dive bar. Melanie was perplexed as to which place she was being taken to. She looked at Kristen in confusion, and her friend could read in her eyes that she had no idea what was going on.

"I thought it would be fun getting a physic reading," she answered to Melanie's questioning look. This wasn't exactly what Melanie had in mind, but she went along with it.

"I suppose it does kind of go with the whole Gatsby theme," she joked to her friend.

The girls entered the shop that was yet another gloomy atmosphere. This place was however a tad bit unsettling to them. Crystal rocks were placed on tables around the room, beads were hanging from the ceiling and tapestry was flowing across walls. A lady stepped out through one of the beaded entryways and bowed her head at them.

"I've been expecting you two. Kristen and Melanie, correct?" Melanie's stomach jumped and she looked at her friend, who was smiling at her reaction.

"Yes. Hello, I am Kristen. I am the one you spoke to over the phone." She reached out to shake the psychic's hand.

The lady took her hand and guided her to the back room. Kristen snatched Melanie's arm to follow. Once they weaseled their way to the back room, there were two cushioned chairs on one side of the table, and her throne of a chair on the other side. The table was covered with a dark red cloth and cards lying on top.

"Please, sit down. I must begin with Melanie. I feel so much energy coming from her world." Melanie's tummy was doing all sorts of flips in nervousness. They sat down, slowly and carefully, almost as if there were needles on the cushions.

The psychic took Melanie's hands and held them, then closed her eyes. She began by talking about Melanie's life growing up, followed by several present-day related things, before discussing a little bit about the future.

During the conversation, she mentioned "I see that your daughter has a sibling." Melanie understood that to mean that she would be having another child, without recognizing that the psychic said "has", already referring to the present tense. Once she completed the reading on Melanie, she moved onto Kristen. Her reading was very similar but presented in another way. It almost felt like a gimmick.

As they left the building holding each other by one arm latched to the other arm, they laughed at the silliness of that situation. The girls did not speak of their readings since it seemed like a prepared presentation.

"Onto the next adventure!" Manuel exclaimed with more excitement in his voice. The next stop was another hidden treasure of a piano bar. More and more cocktails, dancing, mixologists and loud music ringing in their ears as the night continued, bouncing from one bar to the next. It didn't take long for the ladies to open the sunroof in the limo and stand-up in it, shouting out of excitement to all the other party-goers on the streets of the city.

The evening wrapped up a little after one in the morning. Both girls were intoxicated at this point before arriving home. The driver stopped at Melanie's house first to drop her off.

"Kristen, thank you so much for such a wonderful evening! This was one of the best birthdays I can remember in a long time. You are such a wonderful friend!" She sloppily muttered, before kissing her on the cheek and stumbling inside the house. When she entered the house, she staggered up the stairs to their bedroom. Jim was already sound asleep and did not wake up at all to Melanie's loud bangs of running into walls and furniture. She took off her dress and heels, and immediately crashed into bed. In three short seconds, she was already snoring and dreaming peacefully.

Chapter 20

Adriana was finally back to picking up a few local modeling gigs here and there. Her agency offered her bathing suit photoshoots for a local company on the island. It made life much easier for her, balancing being a single mom and the financial responsibilities that ensue from that. Her body had quickly bounced back the more active she became over the months, that it was hard to believe she even had a baby.

Winter was approaching on the island, as some could feel the slight chill in the air. Early one morning, she took Isabella to daycare, so she could attend another photoshoot. After dropping her off, she drove to a secluded area on the island overlooking a cascading waterfall. She didn't even know this little place existed off the pathway. The Director quickly motioned her where to park. He was a tall, handsome man with dark brown hair. As she approached closer to him, she suddenly recognized his face.

As she got out of the car and walked towards him, he called out to her, "Adriana, right?"

"Yes, that's me." He reached out his hand to shake hers.

"I believe we met before. Your face is definitely one that is hard to forget," he said while winking at her.

She blushed and responded, "Why thank you. I do recognize your face too, but I'm not sure where? What is your name?"

Gabriel responded, "You probably remember me as Officer Gonzalez." Adriana tilted her head in confusion, then it suddenly hit her.

"Oh my gosh! You're the officer that came to my house with those papers. Um... yes, I do recall," now, embarrassed by the fact that he was the one that served her with the restraining order papers.

"You can call me Gabriel. Also, don't worry about that whole situation. It happens. As you can see, I'm no longer an Officer. I decided to pursue my passion in directing photoshoots." He grinned at her, and she saw a twinkle in his eye. My oh my, was he a charming man, she thought to herself. He led her towards the photoshoot set-up, then over to the huts where the hair, make-up and fashion designer individuals were situated.

Per the usual, the following hours were getting Adriana all glammed up for her photoshoot. It was a bit nerve-wracking for her to wear those skimpy bathing suits and to be directed by this sexy man, that she had briefly met before in an uncomfortable situation. There was a lot of obvious flirting throughout the entire shoot. It wasn't long before Gabriel asked if he could take her out on a date. Blushingly, she replied faster than she expected to with a yes. All sorts of thoughts were running through her head. They exchanged numbers, and he mentioned that he would reach out soon to set something up.

On her way back to daycare to pick up Isabella, she could not stop fantasizing about Gabriel. It was almost as if he was reading her mind because in that moment he sent her a text.

"Hello beautiful. I may be a bit anxious for this date already. Are you free tomorrow night?" Adriana wanted to keep him on his toes, so she chose not to respond back to him for at least an hour. When she picked up Isabella, she squished her so hard in excitement to see her again. A few hours away felt like an eternity.

Once she made it home, she put Isabella down for a nap before texting him back.

"Yes, I am," she replied with a smiling emoji. Then, she texted her friend Stacy, asking if she could babysit Isabella the following evening as she had a date. Her friend was ecstatic for her and of course obliged.

Adriana could hardly sleep that night, and it wasn't just because Isabella had woken up crying several times. She was extremely excited and nervous for her first date in a very long time. At five that following morning, Isabella began her usual cries that woke-up Adriana. She got up and walked into the nursery to pick her up. Then she kissed her on the forehead and rocked Isabella in the chair for several minutes before they both fell back asleep. Soon after, Adriana woke up and brought Isabella to the kitchen to feed her.

While she was slowly eating her mushed mangos and peaches, Adriana brewed herself some coffee. Although it was winter time, it wasn't normally that cold in Florida. She opened her kitchen window and French doors to the patio for some fresh air. The birds were already chirping to the sunrise.

"Isabella, what should mommy wear on her date tonight?" Isabella looked at her confused and stomped her hands up and down in excitement on the high chair table. Adriana walked into her bedroom and pulled out a few outfits to show her little one.

"Do you like this one, or that one?" She jokingly asked in a baby voice while pinching Isabella's chunky cheeks. Isabella giggled and screeched in excitement. Then made her baby goo goo sounds.

"I thought this outfit was the cutest one, too!" She responded to her baby's sounds, then kissed her on the cheek. She went back into her bedroom and laid out her black skinny jeans on the bed, along with her long sleeve maroon colored shirt and a black and white polka dotted scarf. Although it wasn't that cold to Adriana, it was cool enough to accessorize with a scarf.

Gabriel planned to pick her up around five-thirty that evening to take her to a ritzy Italian restaurant for dinner, followed with cocktails by the water, as the sun was setting. It sounded like one of the most perfect, romantic dates in her mind. Before she knew it, three in the afternoon rolled around. It had already been such a busy and productive day, that she could have called it a night at that point. Yet, the adrenaline running through her blood kept her going for her upcoming date.

After putting down Isabella for her nap, she hopped into the shower for her typical speedy cleaning time and was out in under ten minutes. She decided to curl her hair and get all dolled up for him. Once she finished her hair and make-up, she put on her outfit for the evening and paired it with a great set of heels. Stacy knocked on the door close to four o'clock. Adriana rushed over, and opened it quietly.

Whispering, she said, "Shhh, little one is still sleeping surprisingly." Stacy quietly brushed past her and put her coat down along with her other things.

"Excited for your date? I'm very anxious to meet this Gabriel guy. And you look hot!"

"Excited doesn't even cut it for how I'm feeling," Adriana responded. The girls catch up for several minutes before Isabella started crying.

"No, no. I'll get her." Stacy said while walking away. She carried sleepy Isabella into the living room and put her into the play pen with some toys.

"Her food is in the fridge and labeled for her evening meal." Adriana said to Stacy.

"I know the gist, lady." She smiled back at her.

The doorbell rang a little later and Gabriel was standing at the door with flowers. Adriana opened the door, blushing and beaming from ear to ear. He leaned over to kiss her on the cheek.

"My, you look stunning."

Shyly she responded, "Thank you." Then led him inside to meet Stacy. She put the flowers in a vase, before kissing Isabella goodbye and they were out the door. Their conversation was flowing so smoothly in the car ride to the restaurant, that you would have thought they had known each other for years. "I didn't know you had a little one?" Gabriel queried. "Oh, yes. That is a long story for another day," Adriana replied with a wink. Gabriel pulled up to the valet stand, and accompanied Adriana into the restaurant by holding her hand.

They sat down and were told the specials for the evening before he ordered a bottle of wine for them. Hours of chatter, laughter and smiles followed before he paid the tab and they headed out. He then took her down to this bar by the water, so they could enjoy more cocktails while watching the sunset. Gabriel took his chance as the sun was setting, to lean in for their first kiss. Sparks were flying all around them as their lips connected. The conversation then continued rolling so effortlessly that it was already ten that evening. Adriana was having the time of her life. She did not want the date to be over, but it was rather late for her.

While driving her home, he held her hand then kissed it gently.

"I had such a wonderful time with you this evening. When can I see you again?"

"I did as well, thank you. Well, how about this weekend? I will just need to find a babysitter, depending on what we do."

He smirked at her then replied, "Sounds great. I will figure something out for us." As he approached her house, he stepped out of the car to open her door, then walked her to the door to kiss her goodnight.

The next several months were a smooth ride for these two. They were always so caught up in each other, that often it felt they were in their own world, even when surrounded by others. Their dates consisted of either an outdoor sport together, kiting, taking workout classes, painting and, of course, several different events in the bedroom, too. As a matter of fact, the chemistry they shared was incredible, like nothing Adriana ever experienced with Jim, or anyone for that matter. After a year of dating, the rest became history for these two love birds.

Chapter 21

As the time went on, Adriana and Gabriel became very serious in a short period of time. They were already discussing living together and buying a bigger home. He immediately stepped up to the plate when it came to Isabella.

The Summer breeze was coming to an end and into the Fall weather again. It was the end of September, when Gabriel told Adriana that he wanted to take a drive the next morning to do some exploring.

"What about Isabella babe?" She questioned him.

"I already asked Stacy if she could watch her, and she doesn't mind one bit. I just thought it would be nice and relaxing to do some nature exploring, just the two of us. We haven't done much of that in a while."

"Okay, that sounds nice. What time should we leave tomorrow?"

"I told Stacy to be here super early because I wanted to get out and about when the sun was rising. I was thinking close to six-ish."

"Wow, and Stacy agreed to that? That's so very unlike her to be willing to do such a thing so early in the morning. She definitely appreciates her sleep," she chuckled.

"Well, yeah, I guess so. So, let's set the alarm for early in the morning to be ready by then, sound good?"

"Sure, honey. By the way, should we order in tonight? I don't really feel like cooking."

Gabriel answered back, "You're reading my mind babe. Yes, let's order sushi from that one place we both love."

Adriana reached into one of the kitchen drawers to pull out the menu and handed it over to him. "You already know what I want," she said while walking away. She picked up Isabella and brought her outside to play in the backyard. She had a small playground in her back yard by the water, with a fence installed for safety reasons.

While pushing Isabella on the swing, she glanced out at the water. It was glistening in the setting sun. The rocking motion of the swing, put Adriana in a short daze. She closed her eyes, while her arms continued pushing the swing, and then she saw Jim. He was standing there on the pier, watching her then running towards her. Then gave her a hug and kiss, before telling her how much of a mistake he made. Suddenly, he glanced down to see his daughter for the first time, and hugged her ever so tightly.

Isabella screamed, "Daddy!" in excitement, because she already recognized it was him. As he was hugging her, he looked back up at

Adriana with his piercing eyes, and said "I love you". Those words echoed in the wind as he got up to hug her with Isabella in his arms.

"Mommy!" Isabella shouted. Adriana quickly opened her eyes and recognized she was having another one of her daydreams. How long was I out? She asked herself. Her body had chills, as she could literally feel Jim's touch again.

"What sweetie? Is everything okay?"

Gabriel walked outside towards her. "Babe, what happened? You were pushing the swing over and over when Isabella already got off it. What's wrong?"

"Oh, nothing. I guess I kind of just got lost in one of my daydreams again. I'm glad she's okay."

"Alright. That was just a little concerning to see. Anyways, the sushi will be here in a few minutes. So, come back inside."

As he waved her inside, Isabella ran into the house first. The sushi arrived shortly after they both came inside. Adriana quickly fixed something up for Isabella, too. She sat in her high chair picking at her plate of peas and other softer items with her fingers, while they munched on their raw fish. Once they finished dinner, Adriana cleaned up her high chair and the kitchen while Gabriel gave her a bath before putting her down to bed.

Adriana then went into the bathroom to splash her face with water, and brushed her teeth. Before heading to their bedroom, she went into Isabella's room to kiss her goodnight. She then walked into the bedroom, changed into her pajamas and lay in bed to continue reading one of her self-help books. Gabriel joined her soon after and turned on the television.

"I set the alarm for five tomorrow morning, sound good?" He inquired.

"Sure. I love you, goodnight babe. I know you'll fall asleep by the time your head hits that pillow," she winked and replied to him.

"You know me too well," he responded, before kissing her on the lips and telling her he loved her back.

The alarm loudly chimed in their ears bright and early that following morning. Gabriel had always been a morning person, so as soon as the alarm went off, he was already up and moving around. Meanwhile, Adriana normally snoozed in bed for several minutes before she could get out of bed. He was a loud morning person, though, turning on lights while she was still in bed, or slamming drawers in the bathroom and making a ruckus all over the place. Normally, she was up not too soon after him because of this. After he used the restroom, he went straight into Isabella's room to wake her up. She had her mother's genes, because she was not much of a morning person either. It took several attempts to get her fully awake. Gabriel was helpful when it came to Isabella and took over a lot of the duties. He got her up, changed and fed for the day.

Adriana slowly pulled her body out of bed and into the shower.

"Babe," she yelled out.

"Yeah?"

"Can you make coffee please?"

"Actually, I was thinking we could swing by that café down the road and get some on our way out. Sound good?" He asked.

"Perfect!" She replied, knowing they would be getting specialty coffees instead of their usual home-made coffee, which amped her up even more.

When Stacy arrived, she didn't even knock on the door. Although she had a spare key, she walked right in as the door was unlocked.

"Good morning, you two!" She stated with a rather chirpy voice.

"Wow, you are mighty alert for such an early time in the morning," Adriana said back to her.

"Well, you know, I'm just excited to see you two and that cute little munchkin of yours!" Something seemed different with her that Adriana could not exactly put her finger on.

Adriana and Gabriel finished getting everything together, then said their goodbyes and were out the door. They moved through the drive-thru of the coffee shop and ordered two large lattes to go. While they were driving and sipping their coffee, Adriana looked over at Gabriel and noticed he was sweating.

"Babe, are you okay? Is the coffee making you hot? It looks like you are sweating bullets." He didn't realize it was that apparent.

"Oh, it's just humid, and yeah the coffee is burning me up." He replied, while turning up the air.

They drove through streets, and nowhere near any nature areas, like Adriana thought they were going to.

"Where are we going? I thought we were going to do some nature exploring today? I mean, I thought that was why we are both in athletic attire," she confusingly asked.

"Yes, we are. I just thought it would be nice to explore town a little and grab some breakfast. But first, I wanted to take you up to the top of the lighthouse, so we could watch the sunrise together and sip on our coffees."

"Aw, honey. That sounds so sweet and romantic. We haven't done that in a while." As he parked the car, he grabbed a few things to put in his pocket and took her hand to walk over to the lighthouse. Eighty-eight steps later, they finally made it to the top.

The view at the top was so breathtaking. Watching the sunrise along the ocean was beautiful, no matter how many times she had done it, even after all the years of living there. While she looked around and finished her coffee, she turned to say something to Gabriel before quickly realizing he was down on one knee.

"Adriana, my love. You are the most amazing woman I have ever met in my entire life. I knew there was something about you, on that crazy day I met you only to serve you papers." They both laughed, but she was now laughing and crying. "I could not imagine my life with anyone else but you by my side. Would you do me the honor of making me your husband?"

"Yes! Oh my gosh, is this really happening?" She shrieked while holding her hands up to her face. He opened the ring box to show a beautiful two-carat Princess Cut diamond ring. The ring sparkled in the morning sunlight, and the beams provided its very own spotlight. He got up, took the ring out of the box and placed it on her left ring finger. Then he immediately hugged her in excitement. They were both teary eyed, kissing one of another.

"See, I thought it was best to do this early on, so the entire day together could be spent celebrating. Now, let's go get breakfast and celebratory mimosas!"

They spent the day bar hopping and singing praise over their engagement instead of nature exploring. People in each bar congratulated them by buying a round of shots. Their level of intoxication was through the roof. Eventually, their walking turned into stumbling to each new spot. Adriana almost forgot to text Stacy what happened and to ask if she minded watching Isabella for the rest of the day, so they could continue their celebration.

After she texted her, Stacy replied, "Of course, I will! Also, I knew about the engagement this entire time and helped Gabriel plan it." She then sent a wink smiley face emoji. Laughs, smiles, champagne and excitement were surrounding their souls throughout the entire day. They were on cloud nine.

As the days passed, they had several conversations about their future nuptials. The two of them decided to elope, instead of having a formal wedding at that point in their lives. They agreed to go to the courthouse only a few weeks later, get married, then jet-set to Europe for a honeymoon. Gabriel's parents offered to meet them in New York City to babysit Isabella while they were out of the country for two weeks. Since they will have a long layover there, they decided to stay a few days to sightsee. They wanted Isabella to see the city with them and to also take her to the American Girl Doll store. She had been begging to go there.

Their flight was scheduled to travel into New York, then out to Thailand. Bags were packed over the following days, and they were ready to escape to their first destination in the city.

Chapter 22

As they arrived in the city, they first stopped to the ritzy and old historic Waldorf Astoria hotel. They still had half the day to explore parts of the city, since it was only around noon. After checking into the hotel and unpacking a few things, they went outside to grab a bite to eat at a local organic café, not too far from the hotel. It was a beautiful Fall day in the city. The foliage on the trees were changing to oranges, reds and yellows. Some of the leaves had already fallen to the ground, creating piles in random places. After wrapping up their meals, they decided to take a walk over to Central Park.

All three of them were walking through several back roads and streets to get to the park. They stopped along the way to look around and take in the sights, when out of the blue, in the distance, Adriana saw Jim. He was sitting outside of one of the restaurants with Melanie, and from afar, what appeared from a distance, to be a child. Was that their daughter? Her heart was racing a million miles a minute. Oh my gosh, oh my gosh, oh my gosh! What do I do?! She kept pondering to herself, repeatedly. There was no way at this point that she could avoid him. It seemed like a sign from the universe, although she didn't quite understand what that sign meant in that moment.

"Babe," she quietly said to Gabriel as she pulled his arm to stop him and Isabella from walking any farther.

"Yeah? What's going on?"

Adriana looked him in the eye, with a very serious look. "Remember I told you about Jim?" She quietly mentioned, without Isabella being able to hear her. He nodded his head, with puzzlement in his eyes. "Well, that's him over there," she stated, while motioning with her head in Jim's direction. "With his wife, and apparently their daughter. I know this is completely awkward and strange, but I feel like I need to approach them to say hello. I haven't seen him in years now, and... he has never met Isabella. I'm not saying at all that I want to mention a word of that right now and here, but I want to at least see how they interact in conversation with me."

Gabriel was looking at Adriana feeling quite astonished that she wanted to speak to them. Yet, he was trying to be a supportive husband. "I can't say I understand, but okay."

She kissed him on the cheek, "Thank you. I promise it'll be short and sweet."

She took his and Isabella's hands, and walked toward Melanie and Jim.

"Sweetie, we are going to quickly say 'Hi' to some of Mommy's friends, okay?" Isabella looked up at Adriana with a cute smile and nodded her head in agreement. As they got closer to Jim and Melanie, Jim saw Adriana almost instantaneously. His face turned white, and he leaned over to Melanie to whisper something in her ear before she could see them approaching. Adriana, Gabriel and Isabella were now standing on the other side of the short exterior wrought iron fence from the patio, right across from Jim and Melanie's table.

"Well, hello. We were just in the neighborhood and saw you all from the distance on our way to Central Park, and thought we would stop by for a second," Adriana said with a rather shaky voice.

"Oh, yeah, hello," Jim said, also feeling quite nervous and uncomfortable. The awkwardness grew by the seconds.

"This is my husband Gabriel, and my daughter Isabella." Adriana quickly chimed in. Meanwhile, Melanie was observing everything she was witnessing. Then had a moment thinking how strange it was that her daughter also has the name "Bell" in it. Without delay, it hit her right away. Adriana's daughter looked rather familiar to her. She glanced over at Annabelle, then back at Isabella. Her eyes quickly changed from confusion to shock. An audible gasp came out of her mouth, then, in an instant, she recalled what the psychic told her about Annabelle having a sibling.

They all looked at her right before Jim mentioned, "Ah yes, nice to meet you all. This is my wife Melanie, whom I believe you have met in the past Adriana, and our daughter Annabelle." His throat was now in his stomach as he realized what Melanie had noticed.

"Well, nice to meet all of you. We better be going," Gabriel uneasily stated. As they were walking away, Adriana glanced back over her shoulder to see Melanie immediately arguing with Jim. She turned her head and smirked. That's right asshole. Caught! She said to herself.

Then she became lost in the flood of memories that came crashing down on her emotions in that moment. Seeing him re-opened a wound.

"Jim, do you have something to tell me?" Melanie angrily asked.

"No, why do you ask? I swear I haven't been in touch with her at all over the years!"

"That's not what I'm referring to! We will discuss this once we are home and I put Annabelle down for a nap."

Jim was panicking, and he tried to conjure up a lie to get himself out of this chaos. They finished up their meal in silence, then paid and left right away. The ride home was also in complete silence. It was so quiet, that Annabelle fell asleep in the car seat.

After they pulled into the driveway, Melanie took Annabelle inside to put her down for a nap. She wasted no time in confronting Jim immediately thereafter.

"Speak now, or forever hold your peace. You need to fess up Jim. I have been through too much with you at this point and will not tolerate your lies any further."

He worriedly responded, "I don't know what you want me to tell you. There is nothing that has gone on between her and me in years. I swear!"

"Jim, do you think I'm a fool? I can see the resemblance between her daughter and ours. I seriously cannot believe this," she responded, feeling very upset and disturbed. Now, she was pacing the room, rubbing her temples in confusion. They bantered back and forth, and

Jim continued sticking to his guns that there had been nothing going on. Their fight was going nowhere, so they walked away from each other and took some space.

Melanie went over this in her head, repeatedly, for several days. It was too coincidental for her to just let it go. Deep down in her gut, she felt there was more for her to know. None of this was adding up. She decided to explore while Jim was out of town on his next business trip that he was leaving for the following morning. The elephant remained in each room they were in at the same time, and it was very uncomfortable. Jim knew he wouldn't be getting out of this one as easily as their other disagreements.

After he left for his business trip that morning, Melanie was immediately up and searching around the house. She started with the computer, exploring every little thing she could find first; which turned out to be unsuccessful. The history was deleted on all the webpages and she had no access to his e-mails either. Then she moved on to areas of the house, looking in every nook and cranny, and drawer, reading letters and pieces of mail. She couldn't find anything until, she went combing through his desk drawers, throwing item after item to the ground as if she already knew the evidence would be in there. As one book fell to the ground, amongst the other items, it flipped open pages, and something fell out of it onto the carpet.

Melanie did not notice this at first, until she was cleaning everything back up, to put it all back into the drawers. She saw a square white piece of paper of some sort, which said, "It's a girl". As she picked it up and read the remaining information, she flipped it over to see it was a sonogram, and it was signed "-A". Her heart practically stopped in that one moment.

"Oh. My. God!" She shrieked out loud to the empty room. Her mind and heart were doing flips that she didn't know what to do next.

She took the sonogram and shoved it into her pocket, then flung everything else back in the desk. As she walked out of the room, she picked up her phone to call Kristen and vent to her about everything.

"What?? You have got to be kidding me!" Kristen shouted over the phone.

"Kristen, what the hell am I going to do now?"

"Well, I have one idea you can start with. What if you reach out to Adriana first to confirm this is all true?"

While Melanie was wandering back and forth around the house, she replied, "I thought about that too. But, what if it's true? Then what? I mean, it must be at this point, right? It all makes sense. And meeting her daughter the other day, she looks so much like Jim."

"Let's start with one thing at a time, okay? We will worry about that once you hear from her on the truth." After they finished their conversation, Melanie jumped onto the computer.

The only way she knew how to get in touch with Adriana was to look her up on social media and send her a private message. It didn't take long before she came across her profile on Facebook. Her stomach was uneasy, just clicking on her profile page. Since she was already on there, she decided to stalk all her photos. "Yup, that's Jim's daughter."

She furiously stated out loud, before letting out a sigh. At this point, she wasn't even depressed over his infidelity, but was more so infuriated with Jim. After examining her page, Melanie clicked on the direct message option straightaway. How do I even start this? She uncertainly asked herself.

"Hi Adriana, this is Melanie, Jim's wife (as you already know). Listen, I need to ask you a serious question to ease my nerves. So, I'm just going to come out and say it. Is your husband the biological father of your daughter?" As she re-read her message, she begun overthinking it.

"No, this sounds silly."

"Hi Adriana, this is Melanie. I am nervous to ask you this, but is your husband the biological father of your daughter? I would really appreciate discussing this further, as to why I'm inquiring. Thank you." She re-read the message, and clicked "Send", before overthinking it once again.

Afterwards, Melanie was incessantly checking her Facebook messages throughout the day to see if Adriana had read it. From what it appeared, Adriana still had not checked the message. Over the following days, she kept glancing at her message inbox, still discovering that she had not even opened it. It took Melanie a moment to realize, that people could not see new messages, unless they accepted them, since you are not "friends" on Facebook. She was very disappointed in discovering this, not knowing how she else she could get in touch Adriana.

Each day that passed felt like an eternity, as she did not give up on checking her Facebook in hopes Adriana would accept her message. Finally, after long five days, she received a message back.

"Sorry to just be getting back to you now. My husband and I were out of the country for our honeymoon. And to answer your question; no, my husband is not the biological father of Isabella. I would be happy to discuss this further with you, as there's a lot I need to talk to you about as well. You can contact me here." Then she provided her phone number.

Melanie's heart jumped in her throat. Not only was the physic correct, but it appeared her gut was as well. It didn't take long before Melanie saved Adriana's number in her phone, but she used a different name, just as Jim did so he wouldn't know after he returned home. Right then and there, she sent her a text message.

"Adriana – Hi, it's Melanie." Her stomach was queasy as she waited in anticipation.

Chapter 23

Adriana responded to Melanie right away,

"Hi Melanie. Would you rather chat on the phone? If so, I will be free in about ten minutes."

As much as Melanie did not want to talk to her, she knew it would be best. "Yes, thank you. Please call me when you can." All Melanie could do was sit by her phone, tapping her fingers, waiting for the phone to ring. She got up to use the restroom and right as she sat down to use the toilet, her phone rang. "Of course, she calls now!" She rushed off the toilet to answer her phone.

"Hello..." she answered.

"Hi Melanie, it's Adriana."

"Hey..."

Adriana cleared her throat. "So, listen, I know this is rather uncomfortable for us both, so I'm going to just cut to the chase. I feel like this is the information you are seeking from me. Isabella is in fact

Jim's biological daughter. I sent him a sonogram years ago to let him know, since you all filed a restraining order on me and I had no way of getting in touch. I never heard from him, so I don't even know if he got it or not."

"He got it..." Melanie responded, as she began shaking.

"Oh, okay. Well, I guess he got it, but decided not to step up to the plate and do anything about it. So, I was stuck raising her on my own. And, for what it's worth, I'm truly sorry for everything I did to you a couple years ago. Also, for what I did prior to that. The person I was then, I don't even recognize today. Now that I am a mother, I've changed so much for my daughter. I'm sure you could probably understand on some level, as a mother, too." Melanie sat there in silence, still shocked and speechless. "Are you there?"

"I'm here... sorry. I am just... flabbergasted. It's true. It's real. My gut told me. A physic even told me. And I came across the sonogram several days ago. Obviously, after seeing your daughter, I could see the resemblance. Yet, Jim denied the entire thing. I honestly don't even want to get into how long the affair has gone on with you two at this point..."

"Oh! It ended when you got pregnant. And of course, once the restraining order was filed on me. There really is a lot on that topic, but that's up to you if you ever want to discuss it."

"Right, yeah. Listen, this really is a lot for me to process right now. I'm not even sure how to handle it," Melanie said in an upset tone.

"I completely understand Melanie, and I'm sorry you had to find out this way. I'll let you go think on it and when you're ready, you can let me know if you want your daughter to ever meet her half-sister, or anything at all for that matter. I'm here and an open to all of that. I think it's the right thing to do, but I understand that isn't fully up to me."

"Thanks. I'll be in touch soon." She hung up the phone, and sat there traumatized for a long period of time. Jim was supposed to be home the next day, and she had no idea how to confront him with this news.

Melanie decided to ponder on her thoughts for the rest of the day and to sleep on them overnight. Perhaps the next day she would have more clarity, or at least that was what she was hoping for. She engulfed herself into entertaining her daughter before calling it a night. As soon as her head hit the pillow, her emotions overpowered her. Her whole body could feel the anger and disappointment she felt earlier when Adriana confirmed the news. She drifted off to sleep, only to begin dreaming about her situation.

When she awoke in the morning from nightmares of it all, she quickly became conscious that this was, in fact, her reality. However, she did wake up with feelings of a new perspective. There were ideas floating around in her head to somehow build a friendship of some sort with Adriana and her family, for the sake of their daughters.

"I never thought I would ever see the day of saying something like that," she said to the empty room.

As she was lying in bed, Annabelle ran into the room and jumped on the bed.

"You little goof! Give me a morning kiss."

Annabelle plopped down next to Melanie and kissed her on the cheek. While they lay there, Melanie heard car breaks outside the house. Jim grabbed his suitcase and walked in the house.

"Honey! I'm home. Where's my sweet little Annabelle?"

"Daddy!" Annabelle screamed while running down the stairs to Jim. She ran and jumped right into his arms. Melanie remained lying in bed, not motivated to get up and face Jim with the news yet.

Jim walked up the stairs with his luggage and Annabelle hanging on his back. "Hey babe, you trying to rest?"

Melanie sat up in the bed, "No, I was just taking my time getting up. Listen, we need to talk." She looked at Annabelle, "Sweetie, let's go downstairs and watch Finding Nemo while Mommy gets breakfast started, how does that sound?"

"Yeahhhhh, Mommy!" She screamed. Jim sighed in frustration, thinking What could she possibly need to discuss now? Already forgetting where they left off. Melanie walked Annabelle downstairs and started the movie for her.

"Jim, come down stairs please when you can. Do you want some coffee?"

He rolled his eyes and answered, "Sure."

Melanie fixed Annabelle some breakfast then patiently waited for Jim, while sipping on the ready-made coffee. Once he set his luggage aside and changed into more comfortable clothes, he headed downstairs.

"Do you want cream or sugar?" She inquired.

"Yeah, both." As she poured his coffee, then mixed in the cream and sugar, Jim sat down on a stool at the island. "So, what is it you need to talk about?"

"Do you really have no clue Jim? Did you really think you were going to get away with this? You really are absentminded. Either that or you really just don't care about me."

He was confused for less than a second before realizing what they discussed before he left town for work. As he was thinking over this in his head, Melanie tossed the sonogram picture out and slid it over in front of him.

"Want to explain that? Let's hear the lie you want to tell me on this one."

Jim exhales noisily before saying, "Listen, it's not what you think."

"Oh? Is that so? So, it's not an actual sonogram of a child you have with someone else? Also known as Adriana, the woman whom we just ran into with YOUR other daughter!" She angrily stated in a rather loud whisper, with Annabelle in the room nearby.

"I can explain," he fearfully responded.

"Oh, yes, you most certainly will be explaining, and all of it," she said back in a very straightforward voice. "You owe me every little detail Jim."

The next thirty minutes were spent with Jim explaining the truth of what had happened years before, and about Melanie talking to Adriana to discover the truth. It was rather uncomfortable at the end of the conversation, because neither of them knew what to say next.

"I don't even know if I want to be with you anymore Jim. You aren't the loyal man I once thought you were. To have to work through the infidelity alone took ages, and now this? I just don't know..."

Jim got up, took both of Melanie's hands, and looked her in the eyes before saying, "Babe, I know we have overcome a lot from that, and I cannot apologize enough. That was a big mistake I made, that continues to haunt me. I didn't know how to handle it then and wanted to pretend it never happened. It obviously wasn't the best idea in hindsight." Melanie looked down, with tears welling up in her eyes, shaking her head.

"What do you want me to do about this now? Should we go back to marriage counseling?"

"I don't know Jim, I really don't know right now. I need a few days to think about all this. It's like the never-ending story with you. One thing after the next."

Jim didn't know what to do or say at that point. He sat back down on the bar stool, looking down in despair as Melanie left the kitchen.

Three days passed as they continued their days in silence with each other, going about their lives. It was almost as if the other person wasn't even there. However, that ever present large elephant continued to follow them around from room to room, as if he never left from the week prior. Annabelle was also aware that something wasn't right, since her Mommy was only making dinner for her, and her Daddy was eating frozen meals alone.

Each night since she discovered the truth, Melanie cried herself to sleep. The anger she had previously, has now turned into sorrow. With Jim in the bed next to her before he fell asleep, she would cry in the bathroom while taking off her makeup and brushing her teeth.

"Mommy, what's wrong with Daddy?" Annabelle asked Melanie while walking into her bedroom one afternoon.

"What do you mean sweetie?"

"Daddy hasn't had dinner with us since he's been home. I see him eating alone. Daddy looks sad Mommy, what is wrong? I don't want him to be sad."

Melanie was heartbroken after hearing her daughter say this. She was also concerned that her daughter had recognized something wasn't right. For some reason, she didn't think Annabelle would have noticed that something was off since Jim was out of town often for work.

"Honey, your father is fine. He's just been under a little stress from work. I don't want you to worry about that sweetie." She gently pinched Annabelle's cheeks and gave her a kiss, then took her hand to walk downstairs to Jim.

"Jim, will you please assure your daughter that you aren't sad, and are stressed with work?" She said sternly, giving him a look so he knew what to say in return.

"Oh, yes. Annabelle, honey. I'm sorry you thought something else is going on. Your Daddy has just been stressed about work, but it's all going to be okay. I love you sweetheart. Come give me a hug."

Annabelle ran over to Jim and hugged him very tightly. "I love you Daddy," she said, while looking up at him and into his eyes.

Chapter 24

The sun was rising over the horizon and the birds were chirping in the trees throughout their yard. Melanie was up early, and outside with the dogs. Even Annabelle wasn't quite awake yet. As she sat outside in the rocking chair, watching the dogs chase each other, she calmed her mind so she could focus on specific thoughts.

While getting lost in her thoughts, she saw Buddy chase a squirrel around the yard that had been taunting him. As Melanie smiled watching over the dogs, Annabelle ran outside to chase Bella. The birds quickly flew off as she came running through the yard. Melanie's smile grew bigger and bigger. "Mommy, look at me!" She screamed while chasing off more of the birds that were perched on the fence.

Annabelle came running up to Melanie and jumped right into her lap. "I love you, Mommy."

Melanie snuggled her head into her daughter, "I love you more. Come on, let's go inside and I'll make you some breakfast."

Once they were inside, Melanie started cooking scrambled eggs and bacon. She made enough for all three of them. While she finished the cooking, and Annabelle was watching cartoons, she snuck upstairs.

"Jim? I'd like to talk. Let's take Annabelle to the park after breakfast. We can grab a cup of coffee on the way there and sit down at the park to chat. Okay?"

"Of course, honey." He replied while rolling over and slowly opening his eyes.

Melanie walked back downstairs to finish cooking breakfast. Shortly after, Jim came down with a big stretch and yawn.

"Daddy!" Annabelle screamed while running up to him. Melanie put the three plates of bacon and eggs out on the table as Annabelle and Jim walked over to sit down.

"Annabelle, sweetie, after breakfast we are going to get you changed and head down to the park."

Annabelle looked up at her mother, with a huge, cheesy grin filled with bacon in her teeth. "To my favorite park, Mommy?"

"To your favorite park, sweetheart."

After they wrapped up breakfast, Melanie put all the dishes in the sink to deal with later. Then she took Annabelle upstairs to help her get changed. Once they were all ready to go, they headed out for the morning. On the way to the park, Melanie stopped over at the drive-thru of coffee shop. She ordered a hot latte for herself and Jim, and a hot chocolate for Annabelle.

When Melanie pulled into the parking lot of the park, Annabelle jumped out of the car and ran over to the playground.

"Annabelle!" Jim screamed after leaping out of the car and running after her. As he caught up to her and pulled her to the side, he sternly said, "Do not, ever, jump out of the car like that again! Do you hear me? You could've hurt yourself!"

"Yes Daddy, I'm sorry," she replied with pouty lips and eyes.

After Melanie parked the car, she walked up to Jim holding his coffee while Annabelle continued running over to the playground. "Here you go. Let's go sit over here on the bench," she stated, while motioning with her head. He sipped his coffee, while slowly approaching the bench, dreading the conversation. As he sat down, Melanie didn't wait any longer to express her thoughts.

"Jim, I've been thinking about this non-stop, day-in and day-out. I've decided to do what seems best for our daughter. I want her to meet her sister and build a relationship with her. I don't want to keep this huge secret from her."

"With that being said, for our family and our marriage, we need to go back to marriage counseling. I want to do this the right way, and I need you to put everything on the table from the past and before, for us to move on properly. I cannot move forward with any more secrets or lies, Jim. My heart cannot take any more infidelity, lies or deceit. Do you understand the severity of this all?"

"Absolutely, Melanie. I know I have made some huge, and at times almost unforgiving mistakes, that will take time to move on from and

I understand there are consequences with them. I will do whatever it takes to make this work."

"I want to go to therapy this week, if she can get us in. Then, I was thinking of planning a trip to Georgia, to meet Adriana, and her husband, along with Annabelle. Since that would be about halfway from here to the Keys. Just a short weekend to get to know each other, and the children."

"Okay, babe. Whatever you want, and think is best," Jim responded.

"Well, don't you think that'll be good for the kids, Jim? I mean, they need to know about each other. Not only that, I need to build a relationship with Adriana and build some trust. As well as you and I need to build a relationship with Isabella. There's a lot that needs to be done for this to work out the right way. I'm going to contact Adriana and figure out the plan. Can you contact your lawyers about lifting the restraining order?"

"Absolutely. I actually forgot about that."

"I sure didn't. I'll never forget that traumatizing day," Melanie countered.

Several days later after going to their marriage counselor, Melanie contacted Adriana to explain her thoughts then requested if they were all available for a trip to Georgia. It didn't take long for them to schedule something the following weekend. Melanie booked two separate cabins for them in Helen, Georgia.

Over the following days, Melanie spoke to Adriana regularly to build some type of relationship. Sometimes it was truly hard to believe she was even doing this in the first place. Yet, Adriana seemed to be a different person, constantly apologizing to Melanie over and over and thanking her for the chance. She went on into explaining that she would prove to Melanie, that who she was today, was not the same person she was before. It wasn't as simple as that for Melanie, but it was at least helping day by day.

The day finally arrived for their road trip to the mountains. Beforehand, Melanie had a serious conversation with Annabelle about the trip and meeting her half sister. Annabelle was a bit confused, but excited at the same time knowing she had a sister she could play with.

Once they arrived at the cabin, they lugged all their bags inside and unpacked a few things. It was in the later afternoon, and just as Melanie was going to suggest going into town for lunch, someone knocked on the door. Melanie opened the door to see Adriana standing there with her husband and daughter.

"Hello!" Adriana said with a huge smile, right before she reached in to hug Melanie.

This was stranger than Melanie had anticipated. "Oh, hi. We didn't expect to see you all so soon," Melanie responded.

"Yes, I know. We got into town a little earlier than we anticipated and decided to stop over and say hello. I wasn't sure if you all were even here yet but when I saw the car, I thought we might as well swing by. We were about to head into town to get some groceries."

Melanie nodded her head, "Yeah, actually I was just about to ask Jim and Annabelle about going into town for lunch. I suppose we could join you all."

"Yes, please do! We have plenty of room in our car."

Melanie was already a little lost in her mind with thoughts, but refocused. "Okay, why don't you all come in for a moment, so the girls can meet." As she motioned them inside, she saw Jim down the hallway.

"Jim, come over and say hello to Adriana and Gabriel. Isabella is here as well. Where is Annabelle?" Jim looked back at Melanie, startled that they were already here.

"Oh, hey guys," he responded while waving to them. "Annabelle, come over and say hi to everyone."

After Jim called out to her, she came running around the corner and immediately hugged Isabella before saying, "Hi, I'm Annabelle."

Isabella was a little shyer, but smiled back before hiding behind Adriana. "Hi Annabelle, I'm Adriana and this is Gabriel. Can I have a hug, too?" Annabelle nodded her head, then gave her a hug. Meanwhile, Melanie tried talking to Isabella to get her a little more comfortable.

The shyness slowly faded as the girls gradually became more comfortable with each other. After Jim came over, the awkwardness returned rather quickly. It was hard to not instantly be triggered when Melanie saw him hug Adriana. She felt so uncomfortable and almost went into shock in that moment. Why did I do this to myself? She thought in her mind. It was so obvious he was still attracted to her by the way he was looking at her. Even Adriana was feeling a tinge of anxiety with it all. Melanie tried shaking her thoughts for the girls' sake.

Adriana didn't want to let go of the embrace Jim had on her when they hugged. That was the first time they were close to each other in years. It was so long ago since she felt his touch, that feeling again brought back all the memories they shared together. She realized her feelings had not gone away after all, and she still missed him. Jealousy then took over her emotions and feelings. Why did he choose Melanie over me? Am I not good enough? She's not even as pretty as I am.

Adriana was getting lost in her thoughts as was Melanie. She shook it off as quickly as she realized what was happening to her. Wait, why am I going back to my old ways with this? I met an amazing man and I am so lucky to have him by my side. That is not the life I ever want to go back to. She changed her thoughts to positive ones and came back down to reality, with a smile on her face.

After everyone got acquainted, they stepped into Adriana's car to ride into the small town. "Why don't we grab a small bite to eat, then get some food to barbecue for dinner? How does that sound?" Adriana asked the group.

Melanie and Jim looked at each other for approval before responding, "Sure, sounds good." Once she parked, they all walked through the town a little before stopping in a cafe for a bite to eat.

The conversation was flowing nicely as they discussed how Adriana and Gabriel met, and what they did for a living. Then discussed Jim's business, while the girls colored in the books they were given, all the while giggling with each other. Everything seemed to be going as fine as it could be so far.

Chapter 25

When they wrapped up lunch, they walked over to the grocery store to pick out some items for dinner. They agreed to make hamburgers and hotdogs, since it would be easiest for the kids. In addition, they picked up liquor, mixers and wine. The alcohol was an obvious addition for all of them, as the adults all knew they could use a little something to ease their nerves and the awkwardness.

Once they selected all their items and checked out, they drove back to their cabins.

"Do you all want to head over to our cabin around six-ish?" Adriana asked.

"Sure, sounds good," Melanie responded as Adriana dropped them off. The girls said goodbye to one another before the car door was closed.

As Jim and Melanie were walking into the cabin, Annabelle blurted out, "I like her Mommy! My sister." Hearing those words out loud caused a little uneasiness in Melanie's stomach. Some of this was just a little too surreal for her.

"Good, sweetie. We will see her again in a couple of hours. Let's go inside and take a little nap, then freshen up for later, okay?" Annabelle nodded her head as Melanie took her hand and brought her inside.

Adriana and Gabriel pulled up to their cabin, which was only a five-minute walk from Jim and Melanie's. "Isabella, what did you think of Annabelle?"

She looked over at her mom as she was getting out of the car, "It was fun Mommy. Am I going to see her again?"

Gabriel chimed in, "Of course, sweet girl. They are coming over in a couple hours and we will have dinner with them."

"But Daddy, will I get to see her after this?" Gabriel looked at Adriana to respond to that question.

"Yes, you will. We live far from them, so it won't be as often as we may like, but you all can talk on the phone. Maybe we can video chat with her too." Adriana realized she hadn't spoken to Jim or Melanie about telling Isabella that he was her biological father. That was another huge issue she would have to deal with later. There was already a lot happening at once.

Before they knew it, Jim, Melanie and Annabelle were already knocking on their cabin door. The men immediately got the grill going and popped open a couple beers to kick off the evening. The kids were outside running around chasing one another. The only bit of awkwardness at the time was between Adriana and Melanie. After they opened a bottle of wine, the conversation began flowing smoothly.

Without even realizing it, they were a bottle in and talking to each other like they had known one another for years.

After three beers in for the guys, they came in with the grilled meats. Melanie and Adriana were putting together a salad and a couple side dishes. Everyone seemed to be getting along just fine so far.

"Jim, go tell the kids dinner is ready?" Melanie stated. Jim followed his instructions and headed outside to round up the kids.

Shortly after walking out, he ran back inside asking everyone, "Where did the kids go? I thought they were playing out front?"

Everyone looked at each other in confusion. How much had they all been drinking that they had lost track of the kid's whereabouts? Melanie ran outside to look for the girls but couldn't see them anywhere, either. Adriana and Gabriel followed behind, searching all over the place for them. Suddenly, they heard the girls giggling from the upstairs bedroom window that was opened. Melanie looked up in frustration and stormed inside.

"Annabelle and Isabella, please come downstairs, right now," she shrieked. The girls ran downstairs immediately with their heads down, already knowing they were in trouble.

"Girls, playing a trick like that on all of us is not a funny joke and is very concerning. We thought something happened to you both and we were very worried. Do you understand that it is not funny to play around like that and worry your parents?"

Both girls responded, with their heads still down, "Yes." Isabella ran over to Adriana before Annabelle walked over to Melanie.

"I'm sorry, Mommy," she said, while hugging Melanie's leg.

"It's okay sweetie, let's just be more careful next time, understand?" Annabelle nodded her head.

"Well, now that we are all stone cold sober, shall we eat?" Jim jokingly asked. Everyone laughed and got the dinner table situated. Once they were all seated with food on their plates, and more adult beverages, the jokes and communication continued effortlessly.

Hours passed as they drank more, while the kids were watching television after dinner. The adults didn't pay any attention to the time as they became more intoxicated. When Adriana looked over at the clock, she realized it was getting rather late for the girls to still be up.

"Melanie, I was thinking of putting the girls down to sleep, are you okay with Annabelle staying here for the night?"

Melanie looked over at Jim to see what type of expression he had to that question, but he was too drunk to bother to have any type of opinion from what it looked like on his face.

"Um, sure. I suppose that's fine," she replied, before getting up and assisting Adriana with putting the girls down to bed. The girls were giggling and not at all ready for bed. It required a bit of an effort for both Adriana and Melanie to talk them down for bed. Once the kids were finally down, they walked back down to the table. Their husbands had a deck of cards out when they made it back over.

"How about a drinking game?" Jim asked.

"Just for a little bit, Jim," Melanie replied. She was already quite tipsy and tired. As they sat back down, they started playing drinking games for about an hour before Melanie said she was ready to call it a night.

"Jim, let's head back to our cabin for some rest, okay?" Jim was not ready for the night to end but obliged. They said their goodbye's and walked out towards their cabin. As they were walking, Jim said, "Babe, I left my phone. I'm going to run back and get it and give Annabelle a kiss goodnight. I'll be over there in a second."

He ran back to the cabin and through the side window, saw Adriana cleaning up the dishes. Quietly, he knocked on the door, which startled her for a second. She came over to quietly open the door for him.

"Everything okay, Jim?"

"Yeah, sorry. I forgot my phone. Can I come in for a second and get it?"

"Oh sure, come on in." As he pushed past her, he looked around to see if Gabriel was in sight. It appeared he was already upstairs in bed.

"Where's your hubby?"

"He's upstairs in bed now."

Jim felt a strange pleasure in hearing that, then said, "This is kind of crazy, right? All of us being here. I mean, I can't even remember the last time I saw you. Remember that weekend getaway we had in Napa Valley? Man, that was quite an adventure."

Adriana was thrown off by his remarks. "Yes, I remember. I mean, you abruptly cut me out of your life, so it's not hard for me to forget the last time I remember seeing you. Did you find your phone?" She was in no mood to get into something like this right now.

Jim ignored her jab and picked up his phone from the table, and a glass, then casually brushed his body past hers to put the glass in the sink. The smell of his cologne was intoxicating, triggering several memories for her again. He then intentionally pushed his body up against hers and tried kissing her and caressing her breasts.

"Jim! What the hell are you doing?! Stop it!" She screamed out loud, but also in a manner that wasn't as audible for the kids or her husband to hear.

"Oh, come on babe. Don't act like you don't miss me or the sex we had."

"I have put that way behind me, Jim. You left me, and you disappeared! And you left me to raise a child on my own! I am not the same person I was then. And I am happily married. So please do yourself a favor right now and walk out of this cabin before this gets out of hand. If you have any dignity, then you will do that right now. Otherwise, I will get my husband involved."

Jim looked back at her dumbfounded because he always got his way with her; she has never turned him down before. He sat there for several seconds, deciding, in his drunken state of mind, what he wanted to do. Then he grabbed her ass before running out through the door.

After he left, Adriana sat there in the kitchen, not moving. She stared off into space, and tears rolled down her face. He opened a very large wound for her that took years to heal. His actions triggered more than she had anticipated. After finishing up the dishes, she went upstairs and crawled into bed. When she closed her eyes, she saw Jim again.

When she woke up the following morning, a little hungover, she turned over to see Jim in bed with her. He rolled over and kissed her on the cheek.

"Good morning sweetie."

She sat up quickly and looked down at herself to see if she was wearing any clothes. "What the hell is going on?? How are you here? Where is my husband? Did we have sex?"

"Babe, what are you talking about? You know exactly what has gone on. Why are you acting like this?"

Adriana quivered in fear, as the confusion had taken over her entire state of mind, and, at the thought that she was too drunk to remember what had happened. And to think what could have possibly happened that her husband was no longer there.

"Babe? Why are you calling me babe? Where is Gabriel? Where is Melanie? I am so confused!" She began crying and shrieking loudly.

"Adriana! Adriana! Honey!" Gabriel said forcefully while shaking her. "Sweetie, you're having a bad dream." Adriana woke up startled.

"What were you dreaming about? You were screaming and crying." She was at a loss for words in that moment, but muttered something to him.

"Oh, I don't remember. I just know it was bad. Sorry I scared you." She kissed him, then rolled back over to her side of the bed. As she lay there, she looked at the clock which read 3:05 a.m. That dream felt all too real to her. What did that even mean? She thought to herself.

The following morning, Melanie got up bright and early to walk over to Adriana and Gabriel's cabin. She knocked on the door a few times, until Adriana finally made it down the stairs. Adriana's heart was beating so fast in fear, not knowing why Melanie was over there so early. She opened the door.

"Good morning."

"Hey Adriana, hope I didn't wake you too early. I was coming over to check on Annabelle."

"Oh yes, of course! Come on in. I haven't heard them, so they may still be sleeping, but go ahead and head up there if you'd like. Would you like me to make you some coffee?"

"Sure, thanks." She replied before walking in. "I suppose I can have a cup of that before waking her up, if she isn't up yet."

"Great, I'll get it started. Did you all have fun last night?" She nervously asked, testing to see if she knew of anything.

"Yes, it was fun. We will probably be heading out on the road back to New York in a couple of hours. Looks like the girls had fun, too."

"They sure did! I'm really glad we did this even though it was a very short trip, and I really appreciate you being open to it."

"I'm glad we did, too. We will have to see what we can plan next. Perhaps the girls can chat on the phone here and there."

"That sounds like a great idea. Maybe they can video chat, too," Adriana responded, while smiling.

Chapter 26

Melanie found it interesting that, after returning from their trip to Georgia, she hadn't heard from Adriana at all. She assumed that maybe they were just busy, given that it had only been a week since they returned home from the trip. It just seemed strange since they had agreed to having the girls talk on the phone every so often to keep in touch. She assumed that was going to start the following week, but tried to stop overthinking it.

As the weeks went by, their lives became busy again, with Jim still traveling here and there. Also, Annabelle started pre-kindergarten. Their little girl was growing up so fast. And she was such a social butterfly, already becoming acquainted with several other children at school. Now that she was in school for a portion of the day, it gave Melanie time to do some things for herself.

She had grown tired of not working or doing much for herself anymore, so she got back into her arts and crafts. This time she was diving into woodwork; buying cheap items from garage sales or flea markets. Then she would repurpose each one and re-sell them. Some day she wanted to open her own furniture shop with unique items she had revamped.

Adriana could not figure out how to handle what happened in Georgia, so much so that it scared her to open the door to anything concerning Jim, and especially Melanie. Having seen Jim, and him kissing her, brought back a lot of feelings for her. She was confused and overwhelmed, and it just seemed easier to run away from it all right now.

Isabella kept asking about Annabelle, but Adriana kept coming up with excuses for why they couldn't speak to one another in that moment. She felt terrible for running away like she was, but she didn't know how else to handle it. Meanwhile, Melanie was lost in confusion as to what happened. When Annabelle would ask about Isabella, she had to come up with silly lies since she had no idea what was going on.

Now that it's been months of not hearing from her at all, Melanie was very suspicious, so she confronted her husband. "Jim, did something happen between you and Adriana in Georgia? What is going on? Why hasn't she responded to me in months? And why haven't our daughters talked?"

Since Jim didn't care about his actions or behavior, as usual he brushed it off. He always got away with things. "I have no idea, babe. I guess she doesn't want the kids to stay in touch, after all," he said while shrugging his shoulders.

"That doesn't make sense to me though. She was completely on board with all this and was the one pushing me to get comfortable with it. We had very good communication and everything was fine until the trip to Georgia. I don't know what to say to Annabelle about this. She is confused, as am I. Has she reached out to you?"

"Adriana? No, she doesn't contact me."

Melanie had to make sense of this, but no one was providing her the answers she needed. She called her friend Kristen for advice.

"Hey girl, what's going on?" Kristen answered.

"Hey, just been busy with the furniture shop and all. How are you?"

Kristen replied with a quick catch up on her life. Melanie then inquired, "Listen, is this a good time to talk to you about something? I really need some advice."

"Yes, absolutely, what's going on?" Melanie explained the entire situation that had gone on since the trip and when they returned.

"Do you have any clue why she would disappear now and not return any of my calls?" Melanie asked, confused.

"Well, do you want my honest opinion or just the words you want to hear?"

"Of course, the honesty."

"Okay, well, it seems to me like something happened between the two of them on the trip. Do you recall any moments where they were alone or anything?" Melanie sat there quietly on the other end, thinking over the possibilities. Then it hit her.

"Wait, that night we arrived, after leaving their cabin he told me he had forgotten his phone over there and ran back to get it. I mean, he did leave it over there and he noticed it when we were walking back to our cabin. I don't recall how long he was gone, because I drank too much and was exhausted that I crashed as soon as I got into bed. This really has me concerned now, Kristen. You really think something happened with them again?"

"I mean, I don't know for sure, of course. It's just my opinion based off what you've told me. It does seem kind of ironic and almost planned that he noticed he left the phone over there after you two were almost back at your cabin. Nothing else makes much sense. It may not be the case but given his track record I wanted to throw it out there."

Melanie sat there in silence again, confused and feeling sick to her stomach. "Are you there?" Kristen asked.

"Yes, sorry. I'm just thinking of it all now. I have no idea if something happened between the two of them. We've come such a long way that I'm not sure how I could handle this if something did occur again. He told me he doesn't know why she's doing this. I seriously cannot forgive him anymore if he is lying to me all over again. I don't even know how to find out the truth on this."

"Well, start by asking him, which I know you somewhat already did, but try to read his body language to see if he's lying. If he denies it, I would probably send a message to Adriana, asking her for the truth and go from there. And if that's the case, I'm sorry you're going through this again. I support whatever decision you decide to make. But if you decide to leave him, please know you can come stay with me until you get the situation figured out, okay?"

"Yes, okay. Thank you for offering that to me. I'm going to think this over and figure out what to do. I'll let you know the verdict later." Melanie sighed, said goodbye and hung up the phone. She decided not to wait on this any longer. Immediately, she stormed into the office and confronted him.

"Jim, I need to ask you something, and I need you to be 100% honest with me, okay?"

He looked a bit startled, but not at all in the least concerned. "Sure, what's up babe?" He casually responded.

"I need you to tell me what happened on our trip to Georgia between you and Adriana. I feel in my gut something has happened and that is why she isn't responding to me. Tell me what went on between you two."

Jim didn't think twice before responding, "Nothing happened, babe. I've already told you that. Now can we drop it already? I'm tired of discussing this topic of her."

"What do you want to do about dinner?" Melanie watched his body language very carefully. Something was off. His eye contact wasn't direct. He was perspiring. And his response was very rude and disrespectful, like he was guilty of something since he immediately changed the subject. She decided to play along.

"Okay. Let's order take out tonight."

"Sounds good to me. I'll grab the menu and see what Annabelle wants."

As he reached in the drawer for the take-out menu, Melanie walked upstairs and straight to the bathroom. She stood there, looking at herself in the mirror, as the tears began to stroll down her face. After watching herself cry for a few minutes, she splashed her face with water and pulled out her phone. She began typing out a long-drafted e-mail to Adriana, desperately asking for the truth. She decided she will sleep on it, and then re-read it in the morning before sending it.

It also felt best for her to start thinking of a plan to leave Jim if he was lying to her again. As much as she loved him, she was tired of living her life this way. She couldn't stay with a man that clearly didn't appreciate her or respect her. She'd had enough of the heartbreak and stress. But she was conflicted for the sake of her daughter.

"Babe, what do you want? I'm about to order?" Jim yelled upstairs. Melanie wiped her face with the hand towel and walked out of the bathroom.

"Just get my usual," she replied, as she walked down the stairs.

The rest of the evening was spent in silence between the two of them, which felt very awkward and uncomfortable for Melanie, but not for Jim. He ate his meal, then lay on the couch, drinking a beer while watching football. Melanie did most of the work when it came to Annabelle, as of lately. As per usual, she got her ready for bed and kissed her goodnight.

The following morning, Melanie woke up and realized Jim had crashed on the couch again. She shook her head in disappointment. After she got Annabelle up, they headed downstairs, and Melanie brewed a pot of coffee. Jim was still passed out on the couch, with six empty beer bottles sitting on the coffee table. He woke up as soon as he smelled the coffee.

"Oh, hey babe. I didn't realize I fell asleep out here again."

Melanie didn't respond back. She grabbed herself a cup of coffee and led Annabelle and the dogs outside to play. While out there, she sat on the rocking chair and pulled out her phone to re-read the e-mail she drafted last night. Once she read it over several times, she clicked "Send".

It didn't take long before she received an e-mail back from Adriana. Melanie's heart was pounding hard as she clicked to open it. "Hi Melanie. First off, I'm terribly sorry for ignoring your calls and messages previously. I didn't know how to handle what happened and tried running away from it. Obviously, that wasn't mature or respectful. So, to just put it out there immediately, yes, Jim came on to me. He came back to our cabin to grab his cell phone and began talking about our past. He grabbed me for a kiss and tried doing other things with me, too. I pushed him off immediately and was very upset over it, then asked him to leave."

"As usual with Jim, he never spoke of it and acted like nothing happened. But, from that happening, it stirred up a lot of emotions for me and sent me back to a bad place. I didn't know how to confront the situation or what to do, so I ran. I'm sorry and I'm not sure where to go from here. I don't think it's a good idea for me to be in touch with you all anymore, for the sake of my marriage and my sanity at this point. I hope you can understand and I wish you all the best. Take care." She signed her name, and that was it.

Now it was all on Melanie to decide what she had to do. Regardless of all the counseling, and despite what appeared to be a lot of progress they had made in solving their problems, it was clear that Jim, and their marriage, was a tangled mess. Melanie finally recognized that he will never change his bad behaviors; and she doesn't want to live her life this way anymore. As much as she dreaded doing so, she decided it was time to throw in the towel and call a divorce lawyer to ensure she obtained full custody of Annabelle.

Made in the USA
San Bernardino, CA
02 September 2018